"For you." He handed her the

When she grasped it, his fingers touched hers, igniting an unexpected flame. Taking a deep breath to calm her peculiar reaction to him, she attempted to concentrate on the caller. The person had to be Mom or Dad.

"Allison, I'm not finished with you yet," a low, raspy voice said. "It's only a matter of time."

"What?" she asked, confused at not recognizing the male voice.

"I see you're driving alone these days. Daddy let his little girl out? How sweet of him."

Allison felt her stomach churn and her body shudder. "Who is this? What do you want?"

"Our friend did a lousy job. Bad aim. Next time, your boyfriend won't be around to save you."

Allison dropped the phone, horrified, physically ill. Had the nightmare begun again?

DIANN MILLS lives in Houston, Texas, with her husband, Dean. They have four adult sons. She wrote from the time she could hold a pencil, but not seriously until God made it clear that she should write for Him. After three years of serious writing, her first book *Rehoboth* won favorite **Heartsong Presents** historical for 1998. Other publishing credits include magazine articles and short stories, devotionals, poetry, and internal writing for her church. She is an active church choir member, leads a ladies' Bible study, and is a church librarian.

Books by DiAnn Mills

HEARTSONG PRESENTS
HP291—Rehoboth
HP322—Country Charm
HP374—The Last Cotillion
HP394—Equestrian Charm
HP410—The Color of Love
HP441—Cassidy's Charm

Don't miss out on any of our super romances. Write to us at the following address for information on our newest releases and club information.

Heartsong Presents Readers' Service
PO Box 719
Uhrichsville, OH 44683

Love
in Pursuit

DiAnn Mills

Heartsong Presents

Many thanks to Troy and Kari Marrs for all of their help.

So do not fear, for I am with you; do not be dismayed,
for I am your God. I will strengthen you and help you;
I will uphold you with my righteous right hand.
ISAIAH: 41:10

A note from the author:
I love to hear from my readers! You may correspond with me
by writing: **DiAnn Mills**
Author Relations
PO Box 719
Uhrichsville, OH 44683

ISBN 1-58660-469-4

LOVE IN PURSUIT

Scripture taken from the HOLY BIBLE: NEW INTERNATIONAL
VERSION®. NIV®. Copyright © 1973, 1978, 1984 by International
Bible Society. Used by permission of Zondervan Publishing House.

Cover design by Robyn Martins.

PRINTED IN THE U.S.A.

one

Allison Reynolds's first customer of the day at the local Budget Builder's Store smelled of strong coffee and stale tobacco and had a disposition to match.

"Did you find everything you need, Sir?" Allison asked, flashing the middle-aged, balding man a warm smile in hopes it might melt his icy demeanor.

"I guess so," he muttered, avoiding eye contact. "I really needed a paint stirrer. Wasn't anybody back there to shake up the paint or give me something to mix it with. Don't know why ya'll have that fancy machine if nobody's gonna use it."

"I'm sorry, Sir." Allison produced three wooden paint stirrers from underneath her checkout counter. "Is there anything else, or would you like for me to call someone from the paint department?"

"Naw, just ring me up." He swiped at his nose. Allison proceeded to scan the brushes, paint cans, and paint thinner.

"Is this the best paint you got?" the customer asked. His brows lowered as though he relished the opportunity to pounce on her.

Allison recognized the brand name and knew the various types and grades. "What kind of job are you doing?"

"Rent house," he snapped, staring at a crumpled piece of paper. "I'd have asked back there if anybody had been around."

"Well, Sir," she began, "this is a good, medium-grade, latex paint. It's not our best but certainly not the bottom of the line."

"It'll do." He opened his wallet. "How can you be so happy this time of the morning?" He handed her the cash for his purchases, and she inhaled a heavy dose of his breath.

Allison managed another smile. "I'm a morning person." She wanted to say her joy came from the Lord, but the last time she made mention of God to a customer, she almost got fired.

"Well, good for you." His tone rang with sarcasm. "I'm not. Ain't gonna be either."

She hefted several paint cans into a cart and sacked up his supplies. "You have a wonderful day," she said, and he nodded sourly with a token grin.

Allison stifled a laugh. Some customers challenged her more than others, but she always tried to coax a smile from the cranky ones.

She yawned and stretched. Her watch read seven-ten, and her body ached to claim more rest. Thank goodness no other customers mingled about the front of the store. She welcomed the reprieve before it grew busy. This morning came much too early after spending half the night helping her sister, Susan, nurse her twin sons through a case of flu. Unfortunately, Susan couldn't handle cleaning up vomit and called on Nurse Allison for the job.

Taking a deep breath, Allison glanced about her. The air felt heavy, and for some reason, the hair on her nape bristled. Something bothered her—something she couldn't name or figure out. She neither felt ill nor stressed, but a strange sensation hung like a pendulum between her heart and her mind. *Lord, are You trying to tell me something?*

A moment later she greeted another customer, a familiar, elderly contractor who handed her a ticket for a load of lumber. It amazed her how a man of his age could work so hard every day, but he appeared to love it. His regular visits and habitual manner of seeking her out at the checkout made him one of her favorites.

"Good morning," the older gentleman said, "and how is my green-eyed brunette today?"

"Just fine, Mr. Billings," she replied, taking his ticket. "I see you have your day cut out for you."

"Hard work keeps a man young, I always say." Mr. Billings's gray eyes twinkled. "You know I wouldn't recognize you without your cap and work shirt," he teased and proceeded to pull a checkbook from his shirt pocket.

"Probably not, but one day soon I'll replace these with a nurse's uniform." They'd talked about her plans for a nursing career in earlier conversations, and Mr. Billings always encouraged her. Sometimes she had to pinch herself just to make sure she wasn't dreaming. This time next year she'd be working in a hospital.

"When do you start your last semester?" Mr. Billings asked, once she gave him the total and he scribbled out his check.

"In three months—at the end of August. I would have been done in May, but I couldn't complete my clinical work at the hospital when I broke my ankle. I love my job here, but I'm excited about finishing my education."

"This store will lose a smart and pretty employee. And if some sensible young man persuades you to marry him, I want first bids on building you a house." She laughed and took his check. "You have a deal."

He leaned a little closer her way and whispered, "I'll keep praying for you too."

Waving good-bye, Allison knew she'd see him in a week or two. Customers like Mr. Billings made her job worthwhile.

She'd miss him once she began her nursing career. It was a long time coming. She'd be twenty-six by the time she received her degree.

"Good morning, Allison," the store manager greeted, rushing past her. "I see you're staying busy. Keep it up. I like to see industrious employees."

"Yes, Sir," she replied, amused. The manager never walked at a normal pace or spoke to any of the employees directly. He always hurried and scurried about, but no one knew where. His short, chubby frame and constant movement reminded Allison of the White Rabbit in *Alice in Wonderland*. He even owned a pocket watch.

A couple pushed a cart into her aisle, and Allison turned to assist them. Behind the pair a man caught her attention. He smiled, and she returned the gesture. Good-looking, with gorgeous eyes, but he wore a hideous, heavy metal T-shirt.

❧

Officer Beau Oliver backed his truck from his garage onto the driveway. With a huff, he shifted the truck into park and exited the vehicle to manually lower the garage door. Yesterday he'd disconnected the automatic opener when it refused to respond to his remote. After a lengthy examination of his garage door, he discovered the problem lay in the remote attached to his key chain and not the unit in the garage. What a pain.

His whole body cried out for sleep. Working all night, then heading home in time to shower and change before a meeting with the sarge irritated him. *Not all of us are day-baggers,* he inwardly moaned.

A quick glimpse at his watch revealed he had time to stop at the Budget Builder nearby and replace the remote or purchase a new battery before heading downtown. The day's agenda rolled across his mind. Working undercover for the Houston Police Department demanded every minute of his life. Right now, a huge drug case blasted at his senses. He'd been working on it for months, and every turn in the investigation met with a dead end.

As he drove out of the driveway, he caught sight of his neighbors' recycling bins lining the curb for pickup. "Great," he muttered.

Moments later, after another bout with the garage door, he retrieved his own recycle bins from the garage, set them at the curb, and hurried to the store. Perspiration trickled down his temples, and aggravation seeped from the pores of his skin. Already the humidity proved suffocating, and this early May morning promised a long, grueling summer.

Once on the road, he expelled a heavy breath as traffic slowed to a crawl. Some days the idea of driving a patrol car and wearing a uniform sounded appealing. He eased his truck around to the right shoulder and sped past several cars. *I need to call Mom and Dad tonight. I'm so involved with this case, I've neglected them.* Lately, he couldn't think without deliberating who stood behind a huge narcotics ring.

At the Budget Builder, Beau slipped his pickup into a parking space near the store's exit so he could make a quick escape after checking out. He hesitated. His month-old, green-and-tan truck might get scratched, but he'd have to chance it. Realizing he had thirty minutes to spare, Beau vowed to find a new remote with a battery and be rid of his problem in short order. He stuffed his keys into his pocket, stepped out into the morning sun, and headed for the entrance. Dressed in cutoffs and a heavy metal T-shirt, he looked more like a blue-collar worker than a police officer.

A certain uneasiness swept over him. Some cops called it

instinct, but he'd never bothered to label the feeling. He had, however, always taken heed and kept his eyes open.

Cool air greeted him from inside the huge warehouse-type store. The smell of fresh lumber reminded him of the deck he planned to build on the back of his house. So many projects and so little time. . . He studied the overhead signs to find which aisle contained garage door materials. *Aisle 8,* he read and walked briskly to the area.

"Can I help you?" a teenage boy wearing one of the light blue Budget Builder's shirts and cap asked.

Beau smiled and shook his head. *I wonder how many speeding tickets you have.* Immediately guilt hit him head on for his unkind thoughts. "No thanks, I believe I can find everything myself."

Once he located the garage door openers, he spent five minutes looking for a possible solution to his existing problem. Frustrated and losing patience with the whole matter, Beau reverted to his original thought and decided to purchase a new remote. Before long he wished he'd utilized the young man's offer. There were too many types and options for him, and he was pressed for time. Beau snatched up a small remote similar to the one dangling from his key chain and headed for the checkout.

He'd forgotten a battery, but luckily a display of them in every size and brand stood in front of one of the registers. Instantly Beau spied the correct size and stepped behind the next customer. He glanced up at a young woman behind the checkout and allowed himself a few indulging moments to appreciate the captivating peach-kissed brunette. He liked the way she smiled, and she talked with her eyes—huge, green, endless pools that sparkled when she spoke. They reminded him of the sun glistening atop the water at his favorite fishing lake. He envisioned little flecks of gold dancing off their light.

I wonder if she likes to fish, he mused, imagining the beauty seated next to him in his bass boat. Beau noticed when she laughed, her ponytail bounced. Not every girl looked good in a ponytail, but on her, the no frills or curls approach had an innocent and charming appeal. This way, he could see her entire face framed in caramel-colored hair, and he liked it. He read her nametag. *Hmm, Allison. I wonder if she has a boyfriend. Dream on, big guy. In your line of work, there's no time for a relationship.*

"Good morning," Allison said with a flash of another generous smile. "Did you find everything you needed today?"

"Sure did."

A bearded, greasy-looking man in his midtwenties suddenly caught Beau's attention, and all thoughts escaped him except for the alarm going off inside his head. The man approached the young woman and shouted a string of obscenities. She dampened her lips and attempted politeness, but his voice grew louder.

Beau's every nerve reacted to the scene before him. From the looks of the man's eyes and his erratic behavior, he was either drunk or on drugs—or both.

"Sir, can I get someone to help you?" Allison asked. Her hands trembled.

"No! You're the one I want to see," the man said. "I'm tired of this. Every day I wait for you to come home, and every day you ignore me. Now you're going to pay."

"I believe you have me confused with someone else," she said. "Would you like to talk to the manager?"

Beau quickly laid aside his purchases and stepped forward. "Hey, Man, can we talk about this outside? I've had my fill of trouble with women too." His voice rang calm and controlled while his gaze swept over the man's loose clothing looking for a possible weapon.

The man bellowed another string of curses and claimed his dislike for anyone interfering in his business. From the corner of his eye, Beau saw the other customers move away from the scene, but Allison didn't budge. She looked scared—too scared to move.

"Miss, step away from here," he directed, not once taking his sights off the man. "You know, Man, we can work this out," he continued. "Why don't you tell me all about it in the parking lot?"

"You stay right where you are," the man ordered when Allison attempted to move away from the register. His slurred words convinced Beau of the suspected substance abuse. "And you, get away from me. You ain't stopping me from what I came here to do." The man waved his hands with every word he spoke.

Wishing he had his revolver, Beau cautiously moved toward the assailant in an effort to overpower him. The man clumsily pulled a pistol from inside his shirt, still shouting meaningless threats. Concern for the young woman caused Beau to position himself in front of her. The man aimed and fired repeatedly, pumping bullets into Beau's body. He counted six shots before he slumped to the floor. White-hot pain surged through his side and leg. He tasted the acrid air. Warm blood oozed through his fingers where he clutched his side, and he heard the screams of those around him as he fell prey to utter blackness.

two

The shrill call of the ambulance's siren wailed through Allison's ears, and her heart hammered furiously against her chest. Panic seized her in its grip, choking out her once-comfortable world. An eerie wind whistled around the doors as though a demon encircled the racing vehicle. And the rattle—why did every piece of equipment have to shake? Her mind spun in fear and disbelief. How could this be happening? Surely she'd awaken soon and find her world safe and secure, but the bandaged wound in her left shoulder and the vivid memories of gunshots and blood told her the nightmare had been real.

A paramedic released the blood pressure cuff from around her uninjured arm and called in the reading to a hospital. Hearing the numbers, she cringed. The bottom one disturbed her.

"It's always low," Allison mumbled.

"Your blood pressure?"

"Yes, Sir." Allison opened her eyes and focused her attention on the paramedic adjusting her IV. Brown eyes relayed warmth and compassion.

The hideous bloodstains on her shirt nudged her into another dilemma. *How do I get this out of my shirt? Soak it in cold water and hydrogen peroxide like Mom does? She'll help me. Mom, Dad, I know I'm an adult, but I'm frightened.*

"You're going to be all right, Miss," the paramedic assured

her. "We'll have you at the hospital very soon."

Allison moistened her lips, then bit back the pain searing from her shoulder to her wrist. She tried to concentrate on the muffled voices from the ambulance radio, but instead, tears rolled down her cheeks. She was trained to help those hurting, not deal with her own injuries.

"I know it hurts. I'm sorry, but the doctors don't want you to have anything yet." He adjusted the flow of liquid into the IV. "Just a little while longer. We're headed to Northwest Medical."

She managed a deep breath for courage and strength. Questions bannered across her mind, unanswered fears about her shattered world. "What happened to the man with the gun?" Her gaze darted around the ambulance as though he might be lurking inside.

"You don't need to worry about him," the paramedic said.

Allison closed her eyes. "Yes, I remember. He turned the gun on himself." She didn't think he could have possibly survived. Gritting her teeth, she relived the man firing the weapon into the side of his head. Horror gripped her in a strangling hold.

"The man who tried to help me—" She swallowed the bile rising in her throat. "Is he alive?"

The paramedic took her hand. "He's holding his own."

Allison felt another stab of pain race through her arm. "Thank you," she whispered. "He saved my life."

The fiery wound in her shoulder throbbed incessantly, as though her heart pounded in its place. She refused to give in to the overwhelming sensation to settle into unconsciousness. Not yet. She prayed for the brave man, the frightened people at the store, and the family of the man who shot her. What a waste of human life.

Allison searched the recesses of her mind. She had never seen the gunman before today, and his ravings about her made no sense. Perhaps she should have been kinder, more sympathetic. A sob rose in her throat. Maybe she could have said or done something differently to change the outcome. Except now it didn't matter.

The memories pierced, fresh and gruesome. She again saw the puddles of blood draining life from both men. She remembered staring at her arm, watching the same vital fluid flow from her shoulder, through her clothes, and onto the floor. Now the white bandage seeped crimson.

"Hey, we're almost at the hospital," the paramedic whispered. Still holding her hand, he reached for a tissue and dabbed the wetness from her cheeks.

But you didn't see the hideous, twisted flesh of both men or hear the ghastly screams of the people as they fell to the floor, she wanted to shout, but he had witnessed the scene. He'd been the first paramedic inside the store. The pungent taste of bile again rose and fell in her throat.

"It was so horrible," she said. "I'll never forget it—no never." *Oh, God, why? I don't understand any of this. I know You're with me; I believe You're here. Oh, sweet Jesus, I'm scared. . . . And the man who was shot trying to help me, spare his life, please.*

Allison felt the ambulance slow to a grinding halt, and for the first time, she felt safe.

The hiss of the automatic doors leading into the emergency room and the sterile, antiseptic air jarred her senses. The sights and sounds worried her, because she knew from her nursing education what would happen next. Like a child, she dreaded the procedures. Closing her eyes, Allison sought refuge behind darkness.

"Can you give me some information?" she heard a woman ask crisply.

Allison nodded and felt more tears stream down her cheeks. A burst of agony exploded from her shoulder, and she cried out.

"The young woman's parents have given us enough for now," another female voice stated firmly. "She can sign later."

"Mom, Dad?" Allison questioned weakly. She opened her eyes to look for them, but the paramedics quickly wheeled her through a set of double doors and past several more doctors and nurses all in a haze of colored scrubs. She heard someone bark orders to move out of the way.

A flash of light blinded and momentarily disoriented her, then she realized someone had taken her picture. She closed her eyes to the lights and activity whirling around her, but she couldn't stop the throbbing pain.

"Get away from my daughter!" Allison heard her father shout. The words he spat startled her. She'd never heard him sound so angry.

"Allison," her mother called. Instantly, her parents raced alongside the gurney. Her mother grabbed her uninjured hand, and Allison attempted a feeble smile.

"I'm all right," she whispered, mustering the strength to keep from crying. "I'm fine, knowing you're here with me."

"That's right, Baby," Dad said, his voice cracking with emotion. She saw his lips quiver and his green eyes soften. "You rest, and the doctors will fix you up right away."

Allison wanted to say she didn't hurt—that she'd be going home to her apartment in a little while, but she knew better. Her mind continued to spin with concern over the injured man. "A man was shot trying to help me." She bit her lip against the pain. "Dad, make sure he's okay."

"I will; I promise. The doctors are working on him."

She opened her eyes and searched the round face of the balding father she loved so dearly.

"Hush," Mom said, her blue eyes cloudy with tears. She tucked a strand of silver hair behind her ear and patted her daughter's hand. "Save your strength, Sweetheart. We can talk later."

A nurse stepped forward. "We'll take care of her from here," she said gently. "You folks will have to stay in the waiting room. We'll notify you as soon as we can."

Allison's agony suddenly overpowered her, and she drifted into blackness.

ప్ర

Allison's whole body felt numb. Could this be death? Had it all ended at the hospital? What about the injured man? Her parents? Questions zipped in and around her mind, none with answers. She opened her eyes and, through blurry vision, focused on a woman's face. Forcing her eyes to focus, she saw the woman was dressed in green scrubs.

"Allison, are you awake?" the nurse asked, pronouncing every word distinctly.

She nodded and blinked. "I can't feel anything. Am I paralyzed?"

"No, Honey." The nurse smiled, and provided in a soothing voice, "You've had surgery, and you're in recovery."

Allison's lips felt powdery dry, and her throat hurt. "I'm thirsty."

The nurse glanced up at the IV while checking her pulse. "I can get you some ice chips. That will help. Are you hurting?"

"No." Allison sobbed. "I feel like such a baby, but I can't feel my arm."

The nurse gingerly lifted Allison's uninjured hand and rested it on the opposite arm. "See, it's all there, only bandaged."

Relief flowed through her veins and left a sense of humiliation in its wake. "Thank you. Do you know what happened to the man who was shot?"

"I really don't know. Would you like to see your parents? They're waiting outside, and I know they're anxious."

Allison nodded. They must be worried sick. She remembered their tears and Dad shouting at someone taking her picture.

The nurse stepped to the door. "Mr. and Mrs. Reynolds, you can see your daughter for a few minutes."

Allison attempted a brave smile. She detested the lines of obvious grief and worry etched across their drawn faces. She expected to see Mom's eyes red and puffy from crying but not Dad's. He was always the strong one. "I'm sorry," she whispered. "I've put you through a lot."

"It's not your fault, Baby," Dad replied. She saw his eyes well up, and huge droplets rolled down his cheeks.

"Dad, don't cry. I'm fine." She felt so tired, and although she willed her eyes to stay open, they closed. "Mom, tell him I'm fine. I don't want ya'll upset."

"I'll tell him, Allison. I'll tell him."

❧

Beau battled with the pain raging through his body, a tormenting abyss, as though he battled with Satan and all of his diabolical forces. He begged God for release. In one breath he pleaded for God to take him home, and in the next he wanted to live.

He should have reacted faster to the scene at the store. Maybe that young woman wouldn't have been hurt. . .or worse. He wished he knew, and he summoned a prayer for her and the poor soul who shot them both. Amidst the black swirling confusion, he heard voices and the clatter of metal. Slowly he felt his body succumbing to peaceful numbness, and he eagerly embraced it.

≈

Hours later, Allison woke in a darkened room. She focused on two shadowy figures seated at her bedside. Relief flowed through her as she recognized her parents. "Mom, Dad, I'm awake," she whispered and dragged her tongue over her dry lips.

Instantly the two rose to her bedside. "Are you feeling better?" Mom anxiously adjusted the sheet and thin coverlet around her neck.

"Yes, but I'm thirsty," she replied hoarsely.

Her mother spooned ice into Allison's mouth, then took a separate piece to moisten her lips.

"Thank you," she murmured. "I never thought ice could taste so good." She opened her mouth for another spoonful.

"You look like a little bird," Dad said with a chuckle.

"No worms, please. I don't think they'd set well on my stomach." She took a deep breath. "Dad, I felt you and Mom praying for me."

He laid his hand upon her forehead. "We have a lot to be thankful for tonight."

"God was with me, wasn't He?" She swallowed the lump in her throat before turning her attention to her mother. "Tell me about my shoulder. What did they do to it?"

Mom held her hand lightly. "They removed the bullet and closed the wound."

"Sounds simple enough." Allison forced a faint smile. Time and rehabilitation would mend it just fine.

"You've got an excellent doctor. He took extra care, so the healing should leave a minimum of scarring."

"Good," she breathed. "When can I go home?"

"Whoa, Girl," Dad said. "The doctor wants to keep you a few days for observation. You've lost a lot of blood, and he wants to run some routine tests."

"Sounds expensive," Allison said with a sigh. "Good thing I have insurance. Oh, great," she moaned. "I bet Susan is fit to be tied."

"Why?" her mother asked.

"Remember? I agreed to watch Chad and Christopher while she and Tad went out tonight."

"Oh, they went out all right," Dad said. "Your brothers and sisters are all here at the hospital. They just headed to the cafeteria for coffee."

Allison felt strangely comforted in knowing her siblings had been there. From the initial looks on her parents' faces, they needed support. Oh, how she treasured her family. Without warning, the morning's happenings traversed across her mind.

"Dad, how is the man who tried to help? Did he make it?"

He brushed a loose strand of hair from her cheek and took a deep breath. "He's critical. In fact, they transported him to Hermann Hospital, but he's fighting, and we're praying for him."

She closed her eyes. Without warning, exhaustion swept over her, and her arm throbbed. "I'll never forget what he did for me. I want to see him as soon as I can."

three

Two days later, the doctors dismissed Allison from the hospital. With her left arm bandaged and in a sling and the doctor's orders tucked inside Dad's planner, she stubbornly stood from a wheelchair and walked through the hospital doors with the aid of her parents.

She couldn't remember the sun reflecting so brightly or the sky such a deep shade of azure. The birds sang sweeter, their song soothing her troubled mind, but what she noticed the most was the hint of spring flowers and fresh air teasing her nostrils. The busy sounds of city life buzzed about, and it left a disturbing sadness deep inside her.

"What's wrong, Honey?" Mom searched Allison's face through blue eyes. "Are you in pain?"

"No," she hesitated. "Everything seems so. . .normal, like no one cares about what happened to the man who helped me or the man who died."

"Does the reality of this world frighten you?" Mom asked, placing a comforting arm around her shoulders.

Allison tilted her head thoughtfully. Mom had a way of putting emotions into words. "I think so," she said. "See those construction workers over there?" She pointed to a group of men across the street working on the hospital addition.

Both parents glanced in their direction but said nothing.

"The newspaper said Joe Lopez, the man who did the shooting, worked on a construction crew. I know it sounds silly, but I'm afraid of those men. That's prejudiced and wrong, but I still feel shaky. My nurse's training did not prepare me for this."

Dad opened the rear car door and helped her slide inside. "It's not silly or wrong, Alli. You've been through a traumatic experience, and it'll take awhile to get over it."

"I've got a horrible feeling other people are going to be asking me questions and gawking at me like I'm a sideshow freak."

He reached in to fasten her seatbelt and planted a kiss on her cheek. "They may," he replied, with a sigh. "Folks are naturally curious, and most of them don't think before they ask. Well-meaning friends will want to hear the story, and it'll be up to you to discourage their questions. I'm going to do my best to protect you from newspaper reporters and the like, but I can't be with you all of the time."

Allison smiled sadly, wishing she hadn't voiced her apprehensions. "I'm nearly twenty-six years old, Dad, and I'm sure I'll be fine in a few days. I should be going home to my own apartment instead of staying with you."

"You're not getting out of my sight until I'm positive you're okay," Mom said in her don't-question-me voice.

Allison's mind wandered to the injured man, Beau Oliver. She needed to see him, thank him for saving her life. She'd read the newspaper accounts about the shooting. The pastor at his church had initiated a twenty-four-hour prayer vigil, and his parents pleaded for Christians to pray for their son. Praise God, this morning he'd been taken off the critical list.

But the additional news broadcasts sickened Allison. Reporters made it sound like she was some lowlife who had led the assailant to his demise and the man who helped her to his near death. Dad had phoned the TV station and newspaper office in protest, but it didn't do any good. Joe Lopez might have lived in her apartment complex, but it was huge, and she didn't remember ever seeing him.

Mom's voice broke her thoughts. "Remember how you wanted all of this to be a testimony of God's provision? I have faith God will give you the strength and the words during trying times."

Allison nodded. As much as the memory of the shooting sent a surge of terror to her very being, she refused to bother her parents with all of her fears and disillusionment about the media and what other people thought. Her parents would only fret about her state of mind. She'd handle the gossip, or rather, she'd let it rest in God's hands. Last night she asked Him to take the burden from her mind and to turn the whole thing into something good. God had a purpose, but for now, Allison desperately needed the nightmare haunting her to end.

"I want to see Beau Oliver," she announced several minutes later. When she didn't hear a response, she added, "Dad, nothing is going to change my mind."

"There's something you need to know," he replied, "something the press cannot find out. Beau Oliver is an undercover policeman— off duty at the time of the shooting."

❧

"Okay, Alli. I've pulled some strings to get you here," Dad said as they linked arms in the parking garage of Hermann Hospital. "But you won't have much time." His voice sounded chipper, but Allison heard the uneasiness.

"I realize he's in bad shape, but I can handle it. I'm going to be a nurse, remember?" She smiled up into his warm green eyes and wished she could see the familiar glimmer of laughter.

"I wondered about your career choice after this nasty business." He pointed toward the elevator.

"The Lord has reaffirmed my calling to be a nurse," she assured him, with a lift of her chin. "I'm at an advantage because now I know what it feels like to be a patient."

If only she could convince herself so easily. Her first night home from the hospital had been spent tossing and turning, reliving every hideous moment of the shooting. The doctor had prescribed sleeping medication, but Allison refused to give in to synthetic sleep. Her parents suggested counseling, and she'd agreed that speaking with her pastor might help— but shouldn't her faith in God be enough to sustain her through this?

Dad pushed the "up" arrow and teetered back on his heels. "If I were you, I wouldn't want to ever see the inside of a hospital again."

She wrinkled her nose at him, and for the first time, he laughed heartily. His paunchy stomach jiggled, and she relished the knowledge that she'd caused his mirth.

Once on the elevator, she watched the numbers rise to each floor. Her mind spun with what she needed to say. As of yesterday, Officer Oliver had not regained consciousness. It didn't matter; she simply wanted to see him and possibly relate her gratitude for saving her life to his family.

All too soon, the doors opened, and they were at the nurses' station. A pleasant male nurse confirmed the unconscious state of the patient before authorizing her visit.

"His parents are with him. In fact, I'll walk with you down to Mr. Oliver's room."

Allison suddenly wondered why she had felt so compelled to come. She trembled slightly, and Dad patted her hand. Exchanging reassuring glances, they followed the nurse.

Inside the hospital room, she studied the middle-aged couple seated near the bed. From the looks of the woman's wrinkled blouse and the man's crumpled shirt, they must have been there all night. The nurse spoke quietly to them and both glanced her way. Reluctantly they rose from their chairs and ambled toward the door. Taking a deep breath, Allison approached them.

"I'm Allison Reynolds," she said quietly. "I want to tell you how sorry I am about what happened. Is there anything I can do?"

The couple glared at her. "I don't think so," Mrs. Oliver responded, peering down her nose. "The doctors are doing all they can."

Mr. Oliver wrapped his arm around his wife. "He doesn't need any help from the likes of you. You're wasting your time."

Allison refused to allow their icy demeanor to stop her. Dad had already warned her about hostile feelings.

"I'll only be five minutes," she said. "And I'm praying for your son too."

"Go ahead," the nurse said to Allison with a kind smile. "Mr. and Mrs. Oliver, let me show you where you can get some fresh coffee."

Grateful for the nurse's control of the situation, Allison slipped into a chair next to Beau Oliver's bed. Outwardly he looked stable, but one look at the two IV poles holding six bags of fluids, antibiotics, and precious blood told more of the story.

Dad reached for the hand extending from her sling. She knew his thoughts; the officer had taken her place.

Her gaze took in the policeman's well-chiseled features and strong, firm jaw. Thick, dark brown hair swept back to reveal a widow's peak and hung loosely about his shoulders, and below his high forehead were deep-set almond-shaped eyes and high cheekbones. *I wonder, what color are your eyes?*

A slight ridge formed across the bridge of his nose as though it had once been broken, and she resisted the urge to touch a tiny half-inch scar resting on his right cheek. She envisioned his full lips formed into a smile. Beau's TV picture had not done justice to his handsome features.

"Mr. Oliver," she began softly and leaned closer to him, "I don't know if you can hear me, but I'm Allison Reynolds from the Budget Builders Store. I just want to thank you for saving my life. I'll always remember what you did for me, and my whole family is praying for you. In fact, lots of people are praying." Allison swallowed her tears. What else could she say or do for this courageous man?

"He's a big fellow," Dad whispered. "Muscular. His size will help him fight the injuries."

She nodded. "I want to come here every day until he's well."

Her father squeezed her hand lightly. "I understand, but right now we need to go. Our time is up, and his parents should be returning. Shall we pray for him first?"

She felt the familiar calluses from Dad's years of hard work. Somehow, she'd always thought God's hands would feel the same way.

Dad's deep voice broke the silence. "Heavenly Father, we praise Your holy name and humbly ask that You give the doctors wisdom and guard the life of this brave man. In Jesus' precious name, amen."

She stood and studied the face of the heroic police officer who fought for his life. If only she could do something else for him. Prayer didn't seem to be enough when she ached to do more. Struggling with the emotion burning in her throat, she said, "I want to do whatever I can to help him recover."

"He might not want your help, Alli, and his condition is not your fault."

Allison took a deep breath. Her arm throbbed, and she wished she'd taken the pain medication, but it made her drowsy. "Dad, maybe I do blame myself for this, but I don't have a choice in the matter. He took my place, and I'm determined to help him recuperate."

‌ ❧

Through the murky cloud of a pain-infested world, Beau crept through the shadows to grasp a ray of life. No longer did he wonder if he hovered between earth and eternity; heaven promised no pain. And the fire branding his body had only one origin.

He felt as though his flesh had been ripped from his body. For that matter, maybe it had. He couldn't summon the strength to move his arms or open his eyes to find out.

"Mr. Oliver. Mr. Oliver," a woman's gentle voice said. "Are you awake?"

He stirred. He fought the overwhelming desire to float back into obscurity, a blissful existence.

"Can you open your eyes?"

He felt himself climbing, struggling to reach the top of a bottomless pit. Clinging to the voice of the woman, he grappled with the force sealing his eyes shut. At last he managed to let a slit of light to enter his darkness. He opened his eyes to greet a lovely, Asian woman, her voice sweeter than honey.

"Are you in much pain?"

He nodded and watched her adjust an IV. "This will help. You have a couple of people here who are anxious to see you."

He tried to move his head, but the fierce pounding stopped any movement.

"Lie still, Son," his mother whispered. "Your dad and I will be waiting when you awake."

He wanted to convince her he felt fine, but he couldn't rally the strength. Instead, he managed what he believed resembled a smile.

"The doctors say you're going to be just fine," his dad said. "Good as new in no time at all."

Beau closed his eyes. In no time at all. God had brought him this far; He wouldn't abandon him now. He wanted to ask about the condition of the young woman at the Budget Builder. Her face had swept across his mind even while his body erupted in agony—or could it be he'd seen an angel?

How much time had elapsed? Would he recover completely? Was he paralyzed? Had he lost a limb? Questions. . . and no answers. Beau felt himself fading into a peaceful state of sleep. Already the torment had subsided.

≈

Allison stopped by the hospital every afternoon, although Mr. and Mrs. Oliver clearly disliked her. Her stays were but a few minutes, and she realized those visits were vital to her own healing. Guilt riddled her for the injured officer. Sleepless nights and weary days often reduced her to tears.

The thought of telling Mr. and Mrs. Oliver and the media her version of the story tugged at her, but in light of Beau's undercover work, she refrained from exonerating herself. The fact remained, the shooting looked like it had been partially her fault. Since the assailant died, she shouldered the blame.

On this afternoon visit, Allison learned Beau had regained consciousness early in the morning. He'd been comatose since the incident occurred five days ago, and his pale, emotionless face haunted her day and night. All the way down the hall to his room, she thanked God.

She stole into his room and watched his parents hover over his bed. Standing back, she heard him stir, waited in hopes of hearing him speak, and felt a deep longing inside to know him personally. She believed him to be Christian like his parents, for a green leather Bible with his name imprinted in gold lay on his nightstand.

Still she wondered, what kind of man did undercover work? Were his parents aware? Did he thrive on the adrenalin rush?

Mrs. Oliver's glare, as usual, made her wish she'd stayed home.

"Our son is conscious now," she said. "There's no need for you to continue your visits."

"Who is it?" Beau asked hoarsely.

His mother cleared her throat. "The young woman from the building supply store."

"I. . .I'd like to talk to her."

His mother sized up Allison as though trying to decide what variety of rotten fruit existed in human flesh. Mrs. Oliver gave her a steely gaze, and Allison timidly stepped to the bedside.

Seeing Beau alert and conscious was an answered prayer. Her eyes pooled as prayers of thanksgiving spun through her mind.

"Don't cry," he said, each word an effort for him to speak.

She blinked and swallowed. Every day she'd come here waiting for this moment. "I'm Allison Reynolds, and I want to thank you for saving my life—for taking those bullets meant for me. I'm available to do anything you might ever need as you recover."

"It's not necessary. . .really." Perspiration beaded his brow, and his eyes narrowed.

"Son, you don't need to talk to this woman," his mother said. "You're too weak."

"Yes, I do," he whispered and moved his head slightly toward Allison. "Go ahead, please."

"I need you to know it's important for me to do whatever I can, and I want to tell you that my church, my family, and friends have been praying for you."

He offered a faint smile and cringed as an obvious wave of pain swept over his rugged features. "I. . .felt them; God worked a miracle." He attempted to lift his head, but the strain eased him back onto the pillow. "Your arm. . .is it okay?"

She nodded, willing her tears to cease. Glancing about, she prayed for the courage to say what her heart truly felt. "I know your family needs to visit with you, so I'll be leaving, but I hope you don't mind if I continue to stop by." She paused to find her words. "Mr. Oliver, I didn't know that gunman. I'd never seen him before in my life, and although he did live in my apartment complex, I'd never met him." She gazed into his hazel eyes. "I do have one more thing to tell you. What you did for me is like what Jesus did for us all, and I praise Him for sparing your life. I will forever be indebted to you for your selfless act of bravery." She bent and brushed his cheek with a kiss. "Thank you."

Beau watched Allison leave, an angel in disguise. How refreshing to meet someone sweet and gentle, especially when he encountered so many shoddy characters in his line of work. He'd spent too many hours pretending to be one of them.

His mom followed her outside into the hall. No doubt to thank Allison for her daily visits; however, he didn't under-stand Mom's apparent rudeness.

"That young lady lives her faith," Dad said, staring after his wife. "I'm afraid I misjudged her." His gaze trailed back to Beau. "Son, you look exhausted. Get some sleep now."

Beau could only close his eyes in agreement. Strange how a few words of conversation had worn him out. Allison. . . his own angel. Too bad his life held no room for a woman. He remembered his first impression of her and how he wondered if she'd like fishing. Fat chance. He didn't have time to fish himself. His life was too dangerous. . .too easy to get killed.

four

"Miss Reynolds."

Allison whirled around in the hallway to see Mrs. Oliver hurrying after her. She cringed. What would the woman say now? She'd threatened a restraining order before.

"Can I talk to you for just a minute?" One of Mrs. Oliver's eyes twitched as she rubbed her palms together.

"Sure," Allison replied and stepped aside to avoid colliding with a technician who carried supplies to draw blood. The needles reminded her of Mrs. Oliver's daggerlike glares.

"I owe you an apology." The older woman's hazel eyes brimmed with tears, and she unapologetically let them flow. "I'm so ashamed of the way my husband and I have treated you. You've been faithful in visiting Beau every day since your hospital release, and we've made your stays miserable. I'm very sorry."

Allison viewed the sincerity in Mrs. Oliver's lined face, and compassion seized her heart. "I never intended to upset you or your husband. I simply had to do something for your son to let him see my gratitude." She adjusted the shoulder strap of her purse. "The media reports have been brutal. Given the same circumstances, I would have probably reacted the same way."

"You're too kind, Dear. I hope you continue to visit our son and forgive this foolish mother and father. We've been selfish, unable to see your good heart. We're a Christian family, but we failed to act like one."

Allison's body relaxed, and she felt a smile tug at her lips. "Of course I forgive you, and thanks. Your apology means a lot to me."

ଵ

Days passed, and Allison continued to make her daily trek to Hermann Hospital to spend a few moments with Beau. After the first few times, she drove herself, freeing her father from the drive. Oddly enough, each visit grew longer and longer. She enjoyed Beau's company and loved the sound of his hearty laugh. No longer did his parents condemn her with seething glares but welcomed her. Now, if they were present when she arrived, they excused themselves and allowed her time alone with him.

"Tell me about yourself besides your work at the Budget Builder," Beau said one afternoon. He inched down the hallway with a walker, his third time, and the creases across his brow plus the heavy droplets of perspiration indicated the toll taken on his mending body.

"I have one semester left to finish nursing school, which will start in late August. I'm a bit of a late bloomer when it comes to career, but I'm nearly there." She stopped with him while he took a breath. "By the way, you're doing a terrific job with the walker."

"Thanks. It's whipping me," he said, with a grim smile. "What else about yourself?"

"Hmm. I'm the youngest of five. We're a close family and all live within the Houston area. Our parents are great; they've raised us to love Jesus and instilled strong values of right and wrong. What else. . .I have an apartment on the northwest side of town."

He took another deep breath.

"Don't overdo it," she said, her heart filled with compassion. "This is important to your healing, but your strength has to be built gradually."

He forced a smile. "Thanks, Nurse. If I don't get out of here soon, I'm going to climb the walls." He continued slowly down the hallway. "I live in the northwest area too, and I'm a Christian."

"I thought so when I saw your Bible on the nightstand."

"Do you have a boyfriend?"

She laughed. What an odd question to ask. "Don't have the time or the desire to keep up with one of those. Maybe someday, when I'm settled into my career. What about your life?"

"Boring, and I'm a solo man, one of those married-to-my-job types." By this time they'd reached the end of the hall, where a window brimming with sunlight warmed them. "Must be hot outside." He maneuvered his walker around to retrace his steps.

"Tell me more," she said. "Why is your life boring?"

He chuckled. "I work and I putter around the house."

She avoided asking what he did for a living. She feared it might build a wedge in their new, fragile friendship, and truthfully, she wanted him to tell her. "Any pets?"

"Nope. My crazy schedule wouldn't allow it, but sometimes a big old drooling dog sounds good. What about you?"

She could drown in his hazel eyes, and for a moment those pools distracted her. "Apartment living doesn't lend itself to animals, although I do have a betta fish living in a large glass vase with a plant."

"What is a betta?"

"It's a Siamese fighting fish. Mine's blue and turquoise, really pretty. The odd thing about bettas is, they don't get all their source of oxygen from water and must occasionally rise to the surface for air."

"So the lady likes fighting fish? Is that supposed to indicate something about your personality?" He laughed and she joined him.

"Not really. It was a gift."

"I see. What about sports?" he asked, and she knew their conversation kept him from dwelling on his obvious pain.

"Absolutely. I play softball with my church league, and I dearly love watching baseball and football."

"I'm an Astros and Cowboys fan myself."

By now they were back to his room. He clearly looked like a nap was in order. "Beau, you're tired. I think I'd better go."

He pressed his lips together, then said, "You don't have to baby-sit me."

His tone stung, but she knew patients often developed depression in their recuperation, making them tense and irritable. "I'm not baby-sitting you, simply visiting."

"It's not necessary." He stiffened.

"You're right; it's not, but I enjoy our afternoons together." She refused to cater to his bad mood.

"Don't bother. You have your life, and I have mine."

"All right," she said, drawing her keys from her purse. "Take care." Allison walked away without glancing back.

☙

Dinner came and remained untouched while Beau brooded over his parting comments to Allison. If he meant to deter her from visiting every day, why did he feel so crummy? She'd done absolutely nothing to deserve his bad mood— nothing except spread sweetness into his life. She drove to the hospital each afternoon to visit him, and he looked forward to seeing her. Her laughter rippled over him like a gurgling creek, and those sea green eyes caused funny feelings in his heart.

He could easily fall for a woman like Allison, but as he told her earlier, he lived a solo life. No time for a woman. He'd been there, and relationships didn't work. He'd tell her he was an undercover cop, and as soon as the newness wore off, he'd hear the "can't handle your job" story. She'd cry and say good-bye, like they'd all done before.

He'd be left bitter and disillusioned about the whole love business. Broken hearts never got easier to mend, and he'd decided God didn't want a woman in his life.

Feeling even more sorry for himself, he flipped on the TV, but the sitcoms only increased his sour disposition. Allison's fresh optimism about life intrigued and irritated him at the same time. He'd hate to be the one to burst her Pollyanna bubble with a heavy dose of street life.

If they were together, both of them would have to lie about his job, and she wouldn't know his whereabouts for hours on end—certainly not a fair situation in a relationship.

What am I doing thinking about Allison as though we were involved? I've known her for a handful of days. Must be this hospital and nothing to do is clogging my good sense.

Staring at the phone, he realized he owed her a call. Knowing she wouldn't be back to see him didn't set well, and already he missed her. Beau opened his Bible where he'd placed her number. Apologies were not his forte, but she deserved his best.

She answered on the third ring. "Allison, this is Beau. I. . . a. . .I'm sorry about this afternoon. I acted like a real jerk." For a moment, he thought she wouldn't reply.

"I understand you're bored and want to get out of there,

but yeah, you were rude."

He smiled. Hearing her voice made him feel better, even if she did agree about his behavior. Telling him the truth without hesitation gave her another bonus point. . .not that he was keeping count of her attributes. "I'd like to see you tomorrow—that is, if you haven't filled my slot with someone else."

"Not yet. I'd be glad to come, but not unless you want me there. I'm not a doormat."

She didn't make it easy for him. "Guess I had that coming. I would like your company," he said. "And thanks for not hanging up on me."

Replacing the phone, Beau remembered he hadn't eaten dinner. The food still sat on his tray, covered in cellophane and stainless steel. He lifted the lid cautiously and took a whiff of beef stew. Immediately his taste buds swung into gear.

૨ล

"I can't believe I'm playing Monopoly," Beau moaned, "and getting beat too."

"Relax, the game's not over yet," Allison said with a laugh. She couldn't help noticing the way a lock of his dark hair fell across his forehead. "Besides, you've won every game of Clue."

He jiggled the die for his throw. "I'm supposed to; I'm a cop."

"What's that got to do with detective work?"

"Closely related." He paused. "Did anyone tell you about me being an undercover cop?"

She nodded. "My dad told me when I was dismissed from the hospital. He also said the information wasn't to leak out to the press. I haven't told anyone."

"Thanks. I'd hate to have my cover blown. I'm surprised you haven't mentioned it."

"I didn't know how you might react after the shooting—and the sensitive nature of your work."

He chuckled. "I was off-duty then—no gun."

Allison scrambled for something to say. The incident still lay fresh in her mind, raw and painful.

Compassion spread across his face. "I see you're having a rough time dealing with it. Might be a good idea to seek some counseling."

"My pastor," she replied simply and forced a smile. "He's helping me work through the—" She swallowed a lump in her throat, "the memories. I'm sure they must be worse for you."

He shook his head. "No worse than any of the other messes I've gotten myself into."

She shook the die and rolled it across the middle of the board. The number landed her on the Pennsylvania Railroad, which she owned. "I've lived a pretty sheltered life. Your world is what I've seen on TV and the movie screen."

"So are you into cop shows?" he asked with a wry grin.

"Not in the least. I want to be entertained, not scared to death."

He moved his little racecar forward five spaces, which sent him straight to Jail. "At least that's someplace I've been before," he said. "Can I make one call?"

"No. It's pay up or stay put."

"How about bail?"

She shook her head and tried not to laugh. "Remember the old TV show with the detective who said, 'Don't do the crime if you can't do the time'?"

"I remember, but this is Monopoly, and I'm an injured man."

"The law doesn't accept excuses." She snatched up the die and counted the spaces, landing her in the Jail square. "Pay up, Sister," he growled. "This city runs a tight force."

five

Allison stepped through the door of Beau's hospital room. Every day he grew stronger. . .and more impatient to be released. The afternoon sun highlighted his handsome profile and danced off his dark brown hair, giving it a reddish cast. If she had a notion to be interested, she'd look no further, but she neither welcomed the thought of romance nor had need for it.

He laughed and talked with a sandy-haired man who had his back to her. She paused in the doorway and listened to the guy-talk.

"I remember those impersonations you did of our high school teachers," Beau said with a chuckle. "Got you a regular seat in the principal's office."

"I couldn't help myself," the man replied. "I needed some kind of excitement. What about the time we duct-taped the legs of the star quarterback?"

Allison cringed. She could only imagine the pain of pulling off that tape. What made guys do bizarre things to each other?

"Yeah, I remember," Beau replied with a low chuckle. "We picked on him all of the time. Now, I feel a bit guilty about it. Do you know what he does now?"

"Not a clue. All I remember is we called him Duct."

"He writes and arranges Christian music," Beau said. "He performed at my church a few months ago, and he has six kids. I meant to tell you but forgot."

"Six! I can't believe you forgot to tell me. You were probably on a stakeout and had other things on your mind."

Beau nodded. "Imagine so."

Suddenly Allison felt heat creep up her neck and face. She had no business eavesdropping on their conversation and invading Beau's privacy. Deciding to head to the cafeteria, she turned to leave.

"Allison, wait a minute," Beau said, waving her inside.

The sandy-haired man whirled in his chair and greeted her with a broad smile, dimples and all. "So this is Allison," he said, standing and taking giant strides her way. He extended his hand. "I'm Kieron Bates, and Beau didn't tell me you were this gorgeous."

She laughed. "Pleased to meet you. Sorry to interrupt. I think I'll grab a soda and come back later."

"Not on my account," Kieron said. He had the clearest violet eyes. "I've been here way too long; time I headed home." He swung his gaze back to Beau. "I'll continue to get your mail and stash it in a bag until you get out of this hotel."

"Thanks," Beau replied. "I appreciate you looking after my place. I owe you for this one."

"A steak will do when you're up to it." Flashing Allison another smile, Kieron left with a promise to return.

"I didn't mean to run him off," she said, still feeling the color warm her cheeks.

"Not at all. He'd been here over an hour," Beau replied, clasping his fingers behind his head. "Kieron and I go back to high school days. Lost touch in college, then when I bought my house, I found out he lived across the street."

"He seems very nice, and we all need lots of friends."

Beau's brows narrowed. "Got to be careful in my line of work. Sometimes friends are a luxury."

His words moved her to compassion. "I'm sorry. I never realized your job could be so lonely."

"Hey, sorry to intrude," Kieron said, hurrying into the room. "Did I leave my cap?"

Allison picked up an Astros cap on the nightstand and handed it to him. Kieron snatched it up and sprinted toward the door. He reminded her of a comic strip scarecrow after a flock of crows, and she laughed. As Beau joined her, his gaze captured hers. A warm tingling sent little shivers up and down her arms. Where did this come from?

The phone rang, breaking the magic, and he reached to answer it. She couldn't decide if she welcomed the diversion or regretted it.

"For you." He handed her the receiver.

When she grasped it, his fingers touched hers, igniting an unexpected flame. Taking a deep breath to calm her peculiar reaction to him, she attempted to concentrate on the caller. The person had to be Mom or Dad.

"Allison, I'm not finished with you yet," a low, raspy voice said. "It's only a matter of time."

"What?" she asked, confused at not recognizing the male voice.

"I see you're driving alone these days. Daddy let his little girl out? How sweet of him."

Allison felt her stomach churn and her body shudder. "Who is this? What do you want?"

"Our friend did a lousy job. Bad aim. Next time, your boyfriend won't be around to save you."

Allison dropped the phone, horrified, physically ill. Had the nightmare begun again?

"What's wrong?" Beau asked, sitting straighter in the bed. "Are you all right?"

She studied the tiny lines etched at the corners of his eyes, hoping the concentration relieved the gut-wrenching fear that ravished her senses. "A man just threatened me," she whispered.

Beau grabbed the phone, but the caller had hung up. "What did he say?"

She eased down onto the chair beside his bed. Fright gripped her as though the gunman had stepped into the hospital room and pointed a gun at her. In essence, he had.

"Give me your hand," Beau urged. "Talk to me."

Allison opened her mouth to speak, but couldn't utter a word. She held out her clammy hand and allowed his strength to flow through her. She took several deep breaths while her sights flitted from the doorway back to Beau's face.

"I've got to know exactly what he said."

She took another deep breath. At last, she repeated the man's words.

Beau squeezed her hand lightly, then released it to pick up the phone. Wearing a frown, he pressed the numbers in rapid succession. His hazel gaze captured hers, and again he wrapped his fingers around her trembling hand.

"Sarge, this is Beau. Got a problem down here at the hospital."

"Not me. Allison Reynolds. While she was visiting, she received a threatening phone call." He paused. "No, it came into the hospital room."

A moment later, he replaced the phone and studied her face. "You are to stay right here until my sergeant arrives. He'll need to ask you some questions."

"I've done it again." Chills soared up and down her arms. "I've put you in danger."

"Allison," he began, much more calmly than she felt. "You

have obviously seen something that worries these guys. Can you remember anything?"

"No, nothing," she replied, lifting her chin. She prided herself in being strong and self-reliant and refused to be utterly shattered. "I'd never seen Joe Lopez before he pulled his gun at the store, and I've never been involved with anything or anyone who shaded the law. My life is so routine—I work, go home, attend church, and in late summer, I'll finish nurse's training." She combed her fingers through her hair and whirled to face the window. "Could the man who just called be friends or family of the gunman?"

"Possibly," he said thoughtfully, his tone neither agreeing nor disagreeing.

She stared at the world outside, quiet and peaceful with no hint of turmoil. "How did I get involved with such violent men?" She turned back to him, desperately craving answers.

The firm set of his jaw convinced her she wouldn't hear any of his thoughts about the matter. "I need to get out of the hospital," he muttered. "Being chained to the bed like a helpless invalid won't let me get to the bottom of this."

"What have I done to anger these people?" Hot tears stung her eyes, and she felt as though she'd fallen into a frenzied whirlpool. What happened to her resolve? She felt weak and angry at the same time.

"Would you like to pray?" Beau reached for her free hand again. "We may not understand what is going on, but God does. And we need His peace here."

"Yes, please," she said, through quivering lips.

"Heavenly Father God, we have a big problem with the shooting and now this phone call. Allison is frightened, and I'm angry. Guide us supernaturally, and give us Your peace."

In less than thirty minutes, a tall man sporting thick,

prematurely white hair strode into the room.

"Sarge, this is Allison Reynolds," Beau said, reaching out to shake his hand. "Allison, meet Sergeant Jason Landow."

She saw the strain tug at Beau's facial muscles. He needed to rest, not deal with this upheaval. Once the introductions were completed, Sergeant Landow shed his navy blue sports jacket and veered his attention to her. He asked her to repeat the conversation, word for word.

"And you have no idea who this guy was or his reasons for threatening you?" he asked when she finished. He crossed his arms over a barrel chest.

She shook her head. "No, Sir. I lead a pretty dull life. I've spent hours wondering why the shooting took place, and today's call confuses me even more."

"What about your family?"

His question made her bristle. What did her family have to do with anything? "I'm the youngest of five children. Dad owns a printing business. My oldest brother is a pastor, the other brother works with my dad, one sister is a teacher, and the other is a housewife. We're all boring. Besides," she paused to control her rising anger, "I imagine you investigated me thoroughly after the shooting."

Sergeant Landow chuckled, but she didn't find him amusing. He studied her a minute, causing a flow of self-conscious emotions to snake its way through her.

"Can I have your car keys?" he finally asked.

"Why? I'm quite capable of driving."

"I want an officer to search your vehicle before he follows you home."

She fumbled for her keys and handed them to him. At least her bandaged arm was the left one, and he couldn't complain about her driving ability. "It's parked on level three." She pulled a small notepad from her purse and jotted down her license number along with a description of her blue car. Tearing off the piece of paper, she handed it to the sergeant. She shouldn't be angry with him; he had a job to do—one of protecting her against crime.

Sergeant Landow held the car information while he spoke. "Once you're home, the officer will go through your apartment. This is not an invasion of your privacy, but an opportunity to make certain no one is, or has been, there."

She moistened her lips, wondering if her life had turned into a sick movie. "Then what?"

"We wait and see. In the meantime, do you have caller ID?"

"No, just an answering machine."

"I suggest you don't answer the phone unless you know who it is."

She shivered. "I understand. What about my cell phone? Only my family and close friends know the number."

"That should be safe," Sergeant Landow said. He jammed a hand into his khaki pockets and pulled out a business card. "Keep your cell with you at all times, and if you suspect anything out of the ordinary, call me. You can reach me day or night at that number."

He offered the card, but she couldn't bring herself to touch it.

"Allison, take his card," Beau said. "He can't help unless you follow his directions."

Slowly, she reached for the card, although accepting it meant admitting to impending danger. "I don't plan to tell my family or anyone about this," she said. "They'd only worry."

"Are you sure you don't want to stay with your parents awhile?" Beau asked. "I'm wondering if living alone is wise."

"No," she responded a bit too sharply. "Enough people have been hurt because of me. My apartment is in a good area with a gated entry and constant security. I'll be fine."

"If they want in, security systems won't stop them," Beau said, capturing her gaze. "Be careful, and don't open your door unless you're positive who's on the other side."

Sergeant Landow summoned an officer, who took her keys and car information. A short while later, the officer radioed the sergeant that her vehicle was okay.

"I'll walk you to the parking garage," the sergeant said. He turned to Beau. "I'll be back in a few minutes."

"Allison," Beau urged. "Call me when you get home."

"You might be sleeping."

His eyes narrowed. "Call me."

Too exhausted to argue, she merely nodded and joined the sergeant in the hallway. She wanted to ask questions, nail him down for when her world would be safe again, but the words climbed to the top of her throat and slid back down.

"Miss Reynolds, we're working diligently on the investigation, and we'll do all we can to find the answers to today's threat," the sergeant said, as though reading her thoughts.

"I don't want answers; I want it all stopped and someone thrown in jail." She heard the desperation in her voice, as though someone else uttered the words.

He spoke to a passing nurse pleasantly, as though nothing could possibly be wrong. Allison clenched her fists with a strong desire to scream and beat her fists into his face. *I'm so scared. I can't even find the right words to pray. I thought the nightmare had ended. Instead, it has started again.*

All the way to her car, her mind spun with the threatening call and Sergeant Landow's questioning. She didn't care for the tactics of either one. At her car, the police officer returned her keys.

"Thank you," she said, still shaken.

Sergeant Landow opened her car door, then patted her arm. "I know all of this has been difficult, but I'm sure today must have been a prank call."

Allison refused to acknowledge his utterly ludicrous explanation. She knew better, and so did he.

six

"I don't care what it takes," Beau said, once the sergeant returned from the parking garage. He balled his fist and slammed it into his palm. "Allison needs police protection until this is resolved. I don't believe Joe Lopez simply walked into the Budget Builder and shot her because he was high any more than you do. The threat today proves she's in a lot of danger."

Sarge paced the floor in front of the window. "Aren't you overreacting? Today's caller was just some idiot trying to scare her. He saw the media reports and jumped in on the hype."

"Well, it worked, didn't it? And you and I know he had to put out a little effort to follow her here." He heard his voice rise. "I'm not stupid enough to swallow the prankster excuse."

"I'll get to the bottom of it. We already closed the shooting case, but today's business opens it up again."

"Brilliant," Beau growled.

"Looks to me like you're involved with this girl."

Beau raised up on his elbows. "Whether I am or not is not the issue. She's in trouble, and you're blowing it off!"

Sarge rubbed the back of his neck, the lines on his face speaking volumes.

"What are you not telling me about this case?" Beau asked, reaching to his nightstand and pouring a glass of water.

"It's still under investigation."

"I'm not a rookie, so don't give me that stuff."

Sarge hesitated. "We haven't turned up a thing. The investigation shows the gunman mistook her for another woman when he shot both of you. What happened today is another matter."

Beau's anger was rapidly reaching its peak. "A coincidence? I don't think so. Now, what are you really thinking?"

"The little lady obviously made somebody good and mad, or she lied to us."

⁊

Three hours later, Allison had yet to call Beau. The wait gave him plenty of time to repeatedly go over the phone call. He had a gut feeling she hadn't lied. She'd have to be a good actress to pull off the terror he'd seen on her face. What little he knew about her didn't indicate anything suspicious. Innocent and naïve more closely resembled his angel, a dynamic Christian woman who had gotten caught up in the middle of a vicious crime.

The more he spent time with Allison, the more he liked her. Lately his thoughts were consumed by all the little things about her that intrigued him—the fresh sweetness about her, the intelligence behind those endless pools of green, and her giving heart. Every day she brought light and laughter into the dull world of hospital routine. With Allison, he masked his irritation over the lack of progress in his rehabilitation. His leg hurt constantly, and the wounds in his side weren't healing fast enough for his liking.

He wanted to pack up his few belongings and walk out of that sterile environment and back onto the filthy streets. Strange, he craved clean streets for the citizens of Houston, but he wanted to do the cleaning.

Allison symbolized hope for all those who had ever suffered from a senseless crime. Maybe that's what attracted him to her.

Of course, once the doctor released him and he got back to

work, things would change. She wouldn't occupy his thoughts night and day, and he could focus on his case.

Beau glanced at the clock. She'd been home long enough for the cop to go through her apartment several times. Fuming, he snatched up the phone and a slip of paper with her phone numbers.

After the third ring, the answering machine picked up. *Good, she'd listened to Sarge.* "Allison, this is Beau. If you're there, I'd like to talk to you."

The phone clicked. "Hi. I hadn't called because you looked so tired this afternoon."

"How could I sleep, worried about you?" He bit his tongue to keep from lashing out at her.

"Don't concern yourself with me. Everything here is fine. The officer checked out every nook and cranny."

"This is not a laughing matter."

Silence reigned on the other end of the phone.

"I know," she said, her voice weak. "I'm afraid to leave my apartment and afraid to stay. Next Monday, I'm supposed to go back to work."

"I'm really sorry. I forget you don't live with this stuff like I do, and I'm not being very sympathetic."

"How long do investigations like this last? Maybe if I could mark it on my calendar and see progress—" She stopped talking. "I'm a fool, Beau. I know this could drag out and get very nasty before it's all over."

Beau hated putting her through this, and he couldn't lie to her. Already his feelings for her soared beyond what he believed safe for his solitary world.

"You don't have to say a word," she said. "That man is after me, and I don't know why. The sad part about this whole thing is you've already taken several bullets on account of me, and now he's threatening you. I can't visit you at the hospital anymore. It's too dangerous. The next time, you could be killed."

Beau couldn't believe the absurdity of Allison's statement. "Not a chance," he said with a wry laugh. "I'm the cop here, and we're in this together."

"You must have hit your head during the shooting," she replied. "I don't know how many times I need to repeat this, but your vacation in the hospital is my fault. Remember?"

He'd seen the feisty, independent side of Allison a few times, and he rather liked it, even though her conclusions were ridiculous. "You are the nursing student, and I'm the cop. I'm trained to handle jerks. If that guy was serious, then you don't have a chance without me."

"You're awfully sure of yourself," she said, her voice a level below shouting. "I put my faith and trust in God, not a wounded cop who can't get out of bed."

"Ouch."

"You asked for it."

"So what's your plan, Miss Nurse Detective?"

"That wasn't nice either." She sighed. "I'm sorry. I don't want to argue. Can we call a truce?"

He clenched his fist. Stubborn woman. "As long as you understand one thing. Your specialty is nursing, and mine is police work. And for the record. . .my source of help is God."

"I know."

She sighed, and he seized the opportunity to continue with his lecture. "The truth is, you're scared, and you have every right to be. I'm going to do all I can to find the lunatic who called you today, but I can't be worrying about you not following safety precautions. Are you going to comply?"

"All right," she replied meekly. "I'm listening."

Finally she'd come to her senses. "Number One: I'm working on police protection, but in case Sarge refuses, you don't go anywhere unless I know about it—nowhere alone at night, and your cell phone is to be with you at all times. I mean sleep with it, shower with it. Agreed?" When she failed to reply, he repeated his question.

"Okay. I'll do my best."

"Better than your best. Any more calls like today, and I want to know about them immediately."

"Doesn't sound like I have much of a life," she said. Resistance punctuated every word.

"For right now, no. And one more thing: Keep the blinds and drapes closed in your apartment."

"Do you enjoy giving orders?"

"Yes, especially when it involves saving people's lives. One last request—don't come to the hospital tomorrow."

"Just tomorrow?" she echoed, her tone laced with sarcasm.

"Yes, I plan to get out of here. Enough is enough."

"You're not ready. The doctor won't release you."

Her words stung. "Watch me. You're talking to a determined man, and I will leave in the morning."

❧

Allison considered hurling the phone against the wall and irreparably shattering it. Then no one could harass her. What right did Beau or Sergeant Landow have to dictate her every move? She thought the police would have solved this case by now. Instead, her life had become more complicated and completely out of control. She, the confident, clear-headed one, had exchanged her cool demeanor for a dose of debilitating panic.

Someone wanted to kill her, and she didn't know why.

The policeman had searched through every corner and

closet and declared her apartment safe. How little he knew. Haunting whispers wafted about the rooms, taunting her with cruel laughter and odious memories. Always she saw the blood, and in her nightmares the crimson pools flooded until she swam in a river of red.

Oh, God, help me. I'm so afraid. I can't remember any Scripture, and when I try to read Your Word, nothing makes sense. My mind is paralyzed with fear. What am I to do?

Allison rubbed her shoulders in an effort to dispel the terror surging through her veins. Peace. She craved God's tranquility like a newborn craving his mother's milk. The tears were always a breath away, those uncontrollable moments when she weakened to emotion. Always she feared weeping would push her past the brink of sanity, and she'd never be able to step back into a rational world.

Closing her eyes, she tried to pray, but all she managed was a pitiful cry for it all to be ended. A single drop slipped from one of her eyes, and she hastily wiped it away. Shaking her head, she glanced about the apartment, dreading the shadows ushering in the night. Light—she needed to see. Frantically, she flipped on switches and lamps throughout the rooms.

Remembering her promise to Beau, she closed the blinds in her living room and bedroom. Normally when evening approached, she closed them, except this time the act meant survival. Shutting out the impending sunset and night diminished her chances to be seen by him—whoever he was.

Could she have seen a crime in progress and not realized it? Perhaps the caller had been a friend or family member of Joe Lopez or a man who merely wanted to scare her. Whatever the reason, his tactics worked.

Allison swallowed. She heard a rumble in her stomach and ignored it. Food took a backseat to the problems raging through her mind. Right now she wanted to think. Until two weeks ago, she'd never heard of Beau Oliver. Now her life revolved around him. She dare not breathe or take a step outside her apartment without informing him. A few hours ago, the future looked more optimistic than the present. Now she wanted to crawl into a cave and stay there.

When Beau had held her hand today, she had felt an inkling of something forbidden, a hint of things shoved to another time and place. Her life didn't have room for a man. She had enough complications, and the thought of falling in love made her a bit angry. Yet, if she allowed herself to dwell on Beau, he more than attracted her. His rugged, good looks accompanied by the way he lifted his right brow when he talked, his low, throaty chuckle, and his heart for the Lord all persuaded her to bend just a little. But she couldn't. Once HPD resolved the shooting and the phone call, she'd go back to her world, and he'd venture back to his.

Allison crossed her arms and settled down onto her sofa. After all, her changing emotions could merely reflect her dependence on him. God, not a policeman, was her bodyguard.

Over and over, her thoughts revisited the events over the past month. She stared into a lit candle, now and then inhaling the vanilla pear scent waltzing about the room. The phone rang, echoing around the apartment like a banshee. She jumped and waited for the answering machine to pick up the message. Two rings. Three rings. "Hi Allison. This is your mother, wondering about—"

Allison snatched up the phone. "Hi Mom. What can I do for you?"

"Your dad and I have been talking about your policeman. How is he doing?"

My policeman? When did this happen? "He's not mine,

Mom, and he's doing very well."

"Good. I only referred to him that way because he saved your life. Nothing more."

Allison relaxed and leaned onto a pillow on the sofa. "Oh, I know. Sorry if I sounded sharp. He's wanting to get released, tired of being cooped up in a hospital."

"Honey, are you all right? You sound stressed."

Allison caught her breath. Mom couldn't hear a word of what happened today. "I'm fine. A little tired is all."

"Maybe making the drive to Hermann Hospital every day is taking its toll. After all, you need recovery time too."

Allison forced a smile into her response. "You're probably right, and I don't plan to go tomorrow."

"Would you like to have lunch? What about your favorite tea room?"

Allison squeezed her eyes shut. She refused to risk her mother's safety. She needed to ask Beau about such ventures. "I'm not sure. Haven't gotten my appetite back yet."

"If you change your mind, call me in the morning."

"Thanks, Mom, I will. Thanks for calling, and I love you." Allison laid the phone back into the charger. She hated deceiving her mother, but what choice did she have?

The evening dragged on. More and more, her thoughts turned to Beau. She remembered the warmth in his eyes and his gentle touch earlier in the day. Before this afternoon, they'd laughed and talked about fun things they'd done in their younger years, the awkward awareness of the teens, and the sudden realization of adulthood.

"Rebellion was my middle name," Beau had said. "I spent my high school days sitting in the principal's office and the nights roaming the streets, looking for trouble."

"And you were friends with Kieron then?" she asked, finding it difficult to believe Beau had been a problem teen.

"Oh, yes. We were a pair. Then, one night, a friend of

mine met up with a couple of guys who wanted his tennis shoes. They were high on drugs, and my buddy died from their beating."

Shock and disbelief ruled her reply. Although she'd heard about such things on the news, it hadn't happened to anyone close to her. "I'm so sorry. How tragic."

Beau nodded grimly. "God began to move in me, and on the day of Dave's funeral, I cried my eyes out to my dad. He led me to Jesus Christ as my personal Savior. Before graduating, I felt God wanting me to dedicate my life to ending crime on the streets."

Allison nibbled on her lower lip, remembering the sincerity in Beau's eyes. Tomorrow she'd call and apologize for venting her fear and anger on him. Glancing at her watch, she saw a few minutes left before visiting hours ended. She could call and apologize now.

The sound of his voice soothed her frazzled nerves. "Hi, I just wanted to apologize for earlier this evening. I took out my frustrations on you." Suddenly she felt incredibly foolish.

"You already did, remember?"

"Yeah, but I don't think I really meant it."

He chuckled, and she felt the same tingling as when he'd held her hand. "What makes now any different?"

"I'm feeling more gracious." She laughed and looped the phone cord around her fingers. *Am I flirting with this guy?*

"Truth is I'm glad you called. Real glad."

She shifted uncomfortably, realizing she felt more for him than good judgment dictated. She couldn't allow emotions to jeopardize her carefully laid plans for the future.

Confusion tore at her senses. If she hadn't met Beau under tragic circumstances, would she be losing her heart now?

seven

Beau observed as his tall, thin mother meticulously placed his few belongings into a duffle bag. He had just shoved the stuff in there, but Mom needed to make sure each item had a perfect spot. She'd bought him a new shirt and jean shorts to replace the bloodstained ones from the shooting, although she chose a colorful sports shirt with a button-down collar rather than a T-shirt more reflective of his undercover work. He'd already given one of the nurses his bloody clothes to throw away before his parents arrived. No point in upsetting them all over again. They already had serious doubts about his ability to maneuver about his house and wanted him to stay with them. That would cramp his investigative spirit, and he didn't handle smothering well.

"Hey, Dad, you want to go fishing Saturday?" He picked up a rubber band and pulled his hair back into a ponytail. "My boat's in good shape."

His towering dad glanced up from searching through the drawers one more time to make sure Beau had all of his things. "You gonna feel up to it? I heard the doctor cautioning you about doing too much too soon."

"Sure. I may walk with a limp, but I can still balance myself in a boat and toss out a line. What better way to relax?" He reached across the bed for his cane. "If the fish aren't biting, I can always hit 'em over the head."

His parents laughed over his observation. He started to comment about his mother frying up the fish, but the phone interrupted him in midsentence. He snatched it up, savoring the idea of spending time with his mom and dad.

"You want us to lay off your girlfriend?" a male voice asked.

Beau whirled away from his parents, nearly losing his balance, to face the window. Lightning whipped across the sky, followed by a low rumble of thunder. "Glad you called," he replied, "I'm listening."

"Then stop the investigation."

"I don't know what you're talking about." He tore through the recesses of his mind for a clue to the caller.

"So you want to play games?"

"No, just tell it to me straight. I'm confused."

The man cursed. "We leave Miss Reynolds alone in exchange for you backing off your case."

"So that's what this is all about?"

"Exactly. Are you going to play, or do we continue to shake up the little lady? I'd hate to see the pretty woman hurt again because of you. Next time she might not be so lucky."

"Did you have anything to do with that?" Beau asked as he watched the wind bend the trees and toss debris.

"The ex-boyfriend lunatic? Come on. I'm smarter than you give me credit for."

"I've got to think about this."

"Humph. Don't take too long. I'm an impatient man."

Click. Beau took a deep breath and expelled it slowly. Were the two incidents connected or not?

"Problems, Son?" Concern etched lines around his father's nut brown eyes.

Beau gave him a feigned smile. "Naw. Some guy wondering when I'd be back to work. Can't seem to let a fella rest."

"Well, you need time to recuperate. Can't chase bad guys with a limp," his mother pointed out. She snatched up a tissue and dabbed her eyes. "I sure am praying for you to give up this line of work. Every time I hear a siren, I cringe."

Beau kissed her cheek. "Oh, Mom, you want me to pass up the excitement? What would I do with my time?"

She stiffened her five feet ten frame and wagged a finger in his face. "You were nearly killed a few weeks ago. That's not excitement; it's simply pure stupidity. And if you're looking for something to do, why not see more of Allison? I really like her. Besides, I don't think she'd take your bossiness."

"I'm praying about it all too," he replied gently. *Looks like my cover is blown, anyway.*

છે

After Beau's parents settled him in at home, he bid them good-bye at the door. He waited for their car to disappear down the wet street, then called a taxi to take him downtown to meet with Sarge. The latest phone call held priority over everything for Beau—including his health.

His boss eased back in his chair and tapped a pen on the top of his paper-laden desk. "We've got a problem here, Beau. Someone knows who you are and what you've been doing."

"And believes Allison and I are involved."

"I told you that yesterday."

A muscle twitched in Beau's jaw. "I haven't known her very long. She's not the issue here; it's the joker making the phone calls."

Sarge lowered his eyebrows. "You must have stumbled onto something incriminating, and they're worried. Scaring the girl is insurance to keep you quiet."

"Nice thought, if I knew who to arrest. All I have is what I've heard on the streets. The dealers sell exclusively to those who've worked for them a long time."

"Do you think it's an inside job?"

"The thought's crossed my mind." Beau stretched out his leg. It burned from the day's abuse. He should have popped a pain pill.

"Any idea who?"

"I have a few suspects, but nothing concrete."

"I want a list of names." Sarge pushed a tablet of paper toward him. "In the meantime, you're off the case and taking a lengthy medical leave of absence. That should get our friends off your back and give Allison a little peace of mind. Does she know about today's call?"

"Course not. I want to leave her out of it as much as I can." Beau hesitated. "I know the other day you didn't think there was a connection between the shooting and the threats, but have you changed your mind?"

Sarge shook his head and tapped his pencil faster. "Not sure. The gunman had a record of dabbling in a list of crimes, but nothing that would indicate a key position in trafficking narcotics. Naturally, he could have taken his orders from someone else, but it doesn't make sense. Remember, he targeted Allison with his wild accusations, not you."

"Are you sticking to separate incidents? Because I sure don't believe they are." Beau shifted his leg again and frowned. He wanted the answers now.

"There's no connection. Besides, the caller just denied it. You know the type. If they've done something, they want the credit."

The longer he discussed the two situations, the more Beau felt his temper rising, or maybe the pain in his leg had attacked his logic. "Between you and me, I'm still on the case."

Sarge gave him a wry smile and dropped the pen. "As I said, you're off the case due to a medical leave of absence;

but if you unofficially stumble onto something, keep me informed. I can always arrange for backup. Just be careful and keep an eye out for that girl of yours."

"Friend," Beau said, feeling the strain of his first day out of the hospital. "She's a friend."

ᴥ

The following morning found Allison bored and irritable. Sleep had evaded her, and she'd ended up watching a late movie. Unfortunately, the mystery thriller succeeded in frightening her so that she couldn't fall asleep until nearly five o'clock. At eight o'clock, she awoke to the sound of a storm raging outside. Lightning seared the sky, and thunder crashed like a myriad of kettledrums. The same thing had happened in the movie.

While the roar and flashes of nature surrounded her, she attempted to get some food into her stomach. She poured a glass of orange juice and stuck two slices of stale bread into the toaster. Before it finished toasting, she lost power. Drinking the orange juice, she settled for a speckled banana and a handful of dry cereal. The pitiful breakfast suited her mood, and she conducted her own pity-party right on her sofa.

With the drapes and blinds still closed, she lit a candle and placed it on her coffee table. Its meager flicker looked like a tribute to her depression. She wished Beau would call and let her know if he'd been released.

Staring at her Bible and understanding her comfort lay beneath its pages, she thumbed all the way through from Genesis to Revelation. Every verse she had ever underlined held new clarity and meaning. She turned back to Isaiah, where a verse captured her attention—chapter two, verse twenty-two. "Stop trusting in man, who has but a breath in his nostrils. Of what account is he?"

Okay, Lord, my faith is in You and in Your deliverance.

Chapter seven, verse nine she'd memorized her first year in nursing school when other students pressured her to join them in drinking and partying. Now, the words held even more meaning. "If you do not stand firm in your faith, you will not stand at all."

I understand, Lord. You are in control.

On she read as the prophet Isaiah recorded the words of God in His message to the people of Judah. The Scripture soothed her troubled spirit and assured her of God's provision.

Chapter forty-one, verse ten calmed her the most. "Do not fear, for I am with you; do not be dismayed, for I am your God. I will strengthen you and help you; I will uphold you with my righteous right hand."

Allison realized God had not forgotten her. In this precious book of the Old Testament, He had penned the words to comfort her today. He knew why she'd been shot, even if she might never discover the reason why. And He knew who had threatened her. No matter what the future held, He had it all under control. Beau and Sergeant Landow had given her precautions and instructions to keep her safe. They were trained officers who had her well-being in mind, so she intended to abide by their wishes.

What a blessing to have a Christian policeman like Dean concerned about her! She'd much rather have him on her side than a whole force relying solely on themselves.

The weather subsided, and Sandy, a girlfriend from church, stopped by to visit.

"We need a shopping day before you head back to work," Sandy said. She stood and whirled her whole five-feet-two-inch frame. "I've lost ten pounds, and I'm ready for a summer wardrobe."

Allison laughed. "I noticed as soon as you came in. How does Saturday sound?"

"Wonderful." Her gaze darted about the room, then back to Allison's face. "Why do you have it so dark in here?"

"The storm earlier bothered me, so I shut all the drapes and blinds." Allison detested the lie.

Sandy strolled to the living room window and pushed back the drapes. "The bad weather passed an hour ago, and this place looks like a tomb. You're pale too. A burst of sunshine is just what you need."

Allison held her breath. She couldn't do a thing about Sandy's gesture of friendship. "Thanks. I tend to hibernate since the accident."

Sandy offered her a smile. "I don't want to bring up an unpleasant topic, but do you need to talk?"

Boy do I. "I'm fine, really. The pastor is counseling me."

"How is the man who was shot helping you?"

A wave of peace swept over her as though Beau sat in the same room with them. "He's doing quite well. In fact, he may have gotten to go home from the hospital today."

"Good. Now he can put his life back together. So, is he married?" Sandy's eye twinkled.

"No." Allison laughed. "I'm not interested, and he's pretty dedicated to his work."

"What does he do?"

Allison paused to think a moment. She didn't dare tell the truth. Beau hadn't discussed this with her, and she'd already lied to Sandy about the drapes. The term "undercover cop" now left a nasty taste in her mouth. "He assists people in finding new purposes for their lives."

"Oh, like social work, or is he involved in a ministry?"

"I think a little of both."

After Sandy left, she grilled a cheese sandwich and peeled an orange. For certain, she had to start eating better.

At two-thirty, she wished she'd accepted her mother's invitation to lunch, as much for the company as for a good meal. She couldn't avoid her family until the police department determined the problem, nor did she want to. Beau and Sergeant Landow said to keep them informed—not to isolate herself. It might be too late to have lunch with Mom, but a good chat seemed in order.

"Are you feeling better?" her mother asked when Allison called. "You've been on my mind all morning."

"Yes, I am. During the power outage, I had a good prayer time, and God has given me a sense of peace about all of this."

"Wonderful. I nearly came over."

"Oh, Mom, I wish you had. I was terribly lonely, but Sandy stopped by, and we planned a shopping trip for Saturday."

"Things are on their way back to normal. Once you start work on Monday, that nightmare will soon be forgotten. I'm certain of it because my friends and I have been praying."

I only wish it was over. "Thanks, and tell your friends I appreciate their prayers."

Her mother sighed, obviously relieved. "I'm making vegetable beef soup and herb bread tonight. Would you like to join this old couple for dinner? I might add a strawberry pie."

"Love it," Allison replied. She had plenty of time to contact Beau and relay her plans. "And Mom, about last night— I was rude, and you're the last person I want to catch the brunt of my bad moods."

"Don't worry a thing about it. In your shoes, I'd be a basket case. You just keep your chin up and let us love you."

Allison replaced the phone. Spending time with family and friends had been the highlight of her day. What a real blessing. Scrutinizing her living room, she saw dust and a week's accumulation of newspapers. Perfect. She'd clean before phoning Beau and taking off to her parents' house.

After taking on the job of disinfecting her bathroom with one hand, she pulled down her shower curtain and tossed it into the washing machine. Due to her bandaged arm, the job took longer than she expected. She vacuumed the entire one-bedroom apartment and changed the sheets on her bed. Snatching up a cloth and a bottle of lemon oil from her utility cabinet, she tackled the mounds of dust.

Allison glanced at the answering machine. It flashed a new message. She hadn't heard the phone and guessed it rang while she ran the vacuum. Depressing the play button, she waited in hopes Beau had called.

"Allison." She felt the hair bristle on her neck. "I see you didn't get much sleep last night. I saw the light through the blinds of your bedroom until nearly five o'clock." He chuckled. "You can't run from me; I'm everywhere. You know, like God. You want this to stop? Maybe you need to talk to your boyfriend. We spoke today, and he knows exactly what he's supposed to do."

eight

Allison struggled to punch in the numbers to Beau's cell phone. She could barely read them on the slip of paper he'd given her, for the stinging tears blurring her vision. Twice, she had to start over.

"Calm down, calm down," she whispered. "God's in control." She trembled and glanced out the window where the drapes were still open. She felt violated.

Beau answered on the second ring.

"Beau, this is Allison." She caught her breath and covered her mouth in an effort to stop the hysteria.

"What's happened? Talk to me."

"He just called again," she managed and repeated the conversation.

"Did you erase it from your answering machine?"

She glanced at the flashing light. "No. I thought you'd need it."

"Good girl. I might be able to detect something in his voice that I missed this morning."

Allison swallowed the lump in her throat. "What did he mean, saying he talked to you earlier?"

Beau expelled a breath so heavy she could feel his fury. "He contacted me at the hospital. Right now, I'm downtown talking to the sarge. Do you mind if I stop over? If that guy's watching your apartment, he might even call again while I'm there."

Allison heard his urgency. "My parents are expecting me for dinner."

"No problem. I won't stay but a few minutes."

"Are you feeling up to this? I mean, you shouldn't be driving in your condition."

"I'm taking a taxi."

She hung up the phone and checked the time. After putting in a call to her mother about being a few minutes late due to Beau's visit, Allison eased back onto the sofa and waited. Her mother insisted Beau join them, and Allison didn't have the heart to tell her the truth. No point in upsetting her parents—anxiety didn't solve a thing.

What had her nursing classes said about the value of cool, clear thinking in the middle of an emergency? Those instructions hadn't applied when the nurse was the one knee-deep in trouble.

She sat on the sofa, staring out the window, until early evening shadows crept across her apartment, casting in dappled shades of the western sun. Another day soon to be done. No hint of violence or threats, only streams of light. She needed to close the drapes and blinds, but she felt cemented to the sofa. In the heat of summer, her living room became nearly unbearable, but the cooler months were cozy. At another time, she'd have welcomed the light and hint of summer, but not with the thought of a stalker observing her from some point outside.

Uneasiness crept over her, as though every move was being filmed. She stood and closed the drapes, chastising herself for not doing it earlier. She couldn't bring herself to switch on a lamp but instead lit the candle again. The monster had invaded her privacy, violated the sanctity of her home, and threatened more. Now she had a clearer understanding of the trauma of rape. All the nursing classes in the world hadn't prepared her for this piercing terror. Who was this man, and what had she done to anger him?

An hour later her doorbell rang. Staring at the door, she tried to rise, but her legs refused to move.

"Who's there?" She hoped she sounded braver than the fear pounding against her chest.

"Beau. The taxi followed another car through the security gate."

The sound of his voice brought a mixture of cleansing tears and relief. Her limbs responded, and she fumbled through releasing the deadbolt lock. Seeing him in the doorway brought a new realization, accompanied with overwhelming guilt.

"Beau, you shouldn't have climbed those two flights of stairs!" She gasped at his pallor as he leaned heavily on a steel cane. How had he climbed those stairs?

"Hey, Sunshine," he said, his narrowed eyes and the wrinkling of the side of his nose indicating his pronounced pain.

Allison reached for him. "Why didn't you call up here, and I'd have come to you? You're going to end up back in the hospital at this rate."

"Naw." He grimaced. "I'm a strong healthy male. . . good shape."

She helped him to the sofa. "In good shape as compared to what?"

"Funny," he replied, grabbing the arm of the sofa before allowing himself to sink into the cushions. "If nursing doesn't work out, you can always be a comedian."

She poured him a glass of water and wrung out a washcloth to wipe the perspiration beaded on his forehead. He protested as she dabbed at his face.

"Don't smother me, Nurse Reynolds," he said. "I can do it, myself."

"Hush. When you're feeling better, you can handle it all. Until then, let me practice my skills on you."

He closed his eyes and swallowed hard. "You're stubborn, you know that?"

She smiled. "Thank you. I find some forms of stubbornness highly desirable."

After a few minutes, his breathing slowed, and he reached for her hand. "Aren't you supposed to be somewhere for dinner?"

"Mom knows I'll be late, and you're invited."

He rubbed his chin. "How much do they know?"

"Nothing. The information would be too much for them."

He nodded as if in agreement. "I should go home, but I don't want to. We could talk on the way."

She combed her fingers through her hair. "You're an inch from passing out, and you're ready to tackle the stairs again?"

"I'm hungry." He grinned, but the tightening of the muscles around his eyes told her of his discomfort.

"When did you last take a pain pill?"

"Haven't since leaving the hospital. I had things to do, and didn't want my senses dulled."

"That's the idea behind them—mask the pain and put you to sleep. You should have stayed in the hospital."

He leaned his head back. "I'd worn out the welcome mat. What's your mom cooking?"

She hid her amusement with his change of subject. "Vegetable soup and homemade bread. I suppose you haven't eaten since breakfast either."

"Right. I'm a man on the move."

She didn't like his color, and for a moment she wondered if he would pass out. "Perhaps you should rest a bit more."

"We need to go, but first, I want to hear the recording."

"Beau, this is senseless. You're not a well man."

"Don't argue with a cop," he growled, "but I'll make a deal. You can drug me once we get to your parents'."

He listened to the answering machine tape three times, ejected it from the machine, and put it in his pocket before he appeared satisfied and announced his readiness to leave. Although he protested, Allison helped him down the steps and into her car. In her concern over his condition, she nearly forgot about being watched until she closed the door on the passenger side. Glancing about, she neither saw an unfamiliar vehicle nor any strangers.

Once they pulled onto the street, she broached the subject of the phone calls. "I want to know what he said to you," she said, "all of it—not the Cliff Notes version."

"You're awfully pretty," he replied, "but demanding."

"Comes with being the youngest. Please tell me what he said."

Beau turned his attention to the side window before he spoke. "He'll leave you alone in exchange for me stepping back from a narcotics case I've been working on."

"How is this connected to the shooting?"

"According to him, it's not."

She rolled her eyes. "I'm smarter than that."

"So am I, but Sarge believes they're separate incidents. The problem is, I can't seem to connect them."

She slowed at a stoplight and willed her trembling hands to stop while toying with her next question. "What did you tell him you'd do?"

He lifted a brow. "Worried, are you?"

Her insides crumbled, and her lips quivered. He touched her shoulder. "Hey, I'm teasing here. I'm off the case and taking a ninety-day leave of absence. That should give Sarge time to get to the bottom of this."

Her shoulders relaxed slightly, but with his decision came another realm of questions. "You're walking away from a case?"

"Would you rather continue to live in fear?"

She wished she could see his hazel eyes, but in the evening shadows she could only imagine them. "No. My concern is what you're giving up to accommodate me."

"Just because I said I'm off the case and taking a leave doesn't necessarily mean I'm going to sit at home and watch TV."

She understood exactly what Beau implied and didn't know if she found any comfort in his words.

❧

"What are the odds of an off-duty, undercover cop getting shot up like you did?" Lucas Reynolds asked.

"Lucas," Marge Reynolds said, dropping her fork onto her plate with a clink. "You shouldn't ask Beau such a question. Why, he doesn't even know we found out about his. . .position."

Beau chuckled at Allison's parents' squabbling. "I don't mind you knowing, as long as you keep the information to yourselves."

"Oh, we have," Marge replied, her eyes widening. "We haven't told a soul—not even our kids."

"Good." Beau raised a soupspoon loaded with beef and vegetables to his lips and remembered Lucas's question. "I guess the odds are rare."

"I hear you don't wear a bullet-proof vest when you're working," Lucas added.

Beau caught the shock on Allison's face. "Right. Hard to hide one of them under a T-shirt."

"In any event, we owe you for our little Alli," Lucas said.

Beau took a sideways glance at Allison and saw a slow rise of red. Amused, he reached for his glass of iced tea to drown the laughter gurgling inside him. He liked this family; they reminded him a lot of his own. Someday he might have a wife and a few kids but not anytime soon. When it happened, he'd work a day job, then spend tons of time as a Christian husband and father—not the double life he led now.

Sleep crept over him like a sneaky cat. He'd put off taking the pain medication until they arrived for dinner, and the effects were taking over. His leg and side didn't ache, and he wanted to curl up somewhere and not wake up for three days, but he'd been trained in staying alert and concentrated on the conversation around him.

"Beau," Allison said, her voice gentle as a summer breeze off his favorite lake. "You have to get home before you keel over."

"She's right," Marge said. "Honey, why don't you take him home? He looks a fright and pale too. I'll pack up a piece of the pie and some of dinner so he'll have food for lunch."

Beau's mind registered an alarm. "I don't want her running around at night. As soon as we get back to her apartment, I'll call a cab."

"I won't hear of it," Lucas said. "I'll run you home as soon as you're ready."

Beau pushed aside any muddled thoughts. "Sir, I appreciate your offer, but I want to see Allison home safely first. It's a thing with me—you don't take advantage of a lady inviting you to dinner."

Lucas slowly nodded. "For a minute I forgot about what happened. I'll follow you two over, escort my little girl to her apartment, and take you home."

Beau smiled. Not the optimum solution, but it served his

purpose. At least he'd have a few moments alone with Allison in the car. He thanked Marge for the delicious meal and stood, ready to finish up the evening and crawl into bed. If he sat there much longer, he might fall face-first into his soup bowl. He hadn't done that since he was a kid, and he had no intentions of doing so now.

"I'm sorry," he whispered once he and Allison were on their way. "I didn't mean to spoil your evening."

"You need to be in bed, and I'm a poor nurse to allow all this activity."

"You see; I had to see this beautiful lady."

"Pleeeze," she said. "You're under the influence, remember?"

He wet his lips and took a few deep breaths. For now the annoying urge to sleep would have to wait. He hated the way medicine affected him. "I'll call you in the morning and make sure everything is okay." His cell phone rang, interrupting his broken train of thought. Yanking it out of his pants pocket, he saw "caller ID unavailable." Beau mumbled a hello.

"Good work, Cop. You follow orders better than most."

"So you found out I'm off the case and taking a leave of absence."

Allison stiffened, but he needed to concentrate on the caller.

"Oughta give you lots of time with your pretty girlfriend. Oh, by the way, you had a hard time making it up her steps tonight. Thought for a minute you might need some help." He laughed low.

"Glad you're amused at my expense."

"Just remember. One slipup, and Miss Allison will pay. Got it?"

"Sure. I'm keeping my end of the deal." Beau slid the phone back into his pocket. He reached across the seat and laid his hand on her shoulder. "Relax. He won't be bothering you anymore."

She breathed sharply, and he heard a sob. "But you didn't tell him you'd unofficially work at home, did you?"

"The secret is to let them think you are doing exactly what they want."

nine

Allison took in a deep breath before she unleashed her anger and fright. "You're playing with my life. How can you do that with a clear conscience?"

"It'll be all right," Beau said, much too gentle to her liking. "Only the sarge will know I'm tinkering with the case at home. Another cop has already been assigned to the streets."

She stopped at a yellow light and stared into the dark surroundings as though the faceless man with the raspy voice might try to pull her from the car. "I hate this," she said, banging her palm against the steering wheel. "Everything I once took for granted has exploded in my face. I'm afraid for myself and those I care about."

"Allison, you're no longer in danger," Beau said. "I gave them what they wanted. They were trying to get to me, not you."

"Right," she muttered. They sat in silence until the light changed, and she stepped on the gas a little harder than she intended. The car sped away, tires squealing and most likely leaving a patch of rubber behind them.

Two more turns, and she pulled up to the security gate of her apartment complex. Punching in her code, she crept through the entrance to her building. Her dad's convertible wasn't behind them, but he knew her security numbers. She swung into her parking slot and turned off the engine.

"Dad drives slower than I do," she said, avoiding his piercing stare.

"Most people do," he replied, but she didn't appreciate his dry sense of humor at her expense.

"I'm nervous, okay?" She leaned her head on her hands against the steering wheel. The sobs started, and she couldn't stop them.

Beau's hand caressed her shoulder, and as angry as she felt at him for duping the man who had frightened her beyond imagination, his touch felt comforting.

"Scoot over here by me," he whispered.

"I can't," she said. "I might not be able to stop crying, and Dad will be here any minute."

"And he won't understand you're upset after all you've been through?"

"He and Mom think I'm the pillar of strength," she said, sniffing.

"I imagine he knows the real you—his little girl." He massaged her tight neck muscles, reducing the stress ripping through her.

She shook her head and felt her nose dripping over her upper lip like a four year old. She yanked a tissue from a box between them and wiped her nose while more tears flooded her eyes. Beau wrapped his arm around her shoulders and urged her to lay her head against his chest. She wanted his embrace to cease the flow of tears, but it even made her cry harder. Finally the weeping subsided, and she glanced up at the silhouette of his rugged features. She mentally traced the outline of his square jaw, remembering how close to death he'd been because of her. Of course he needed to find those drug dealers. Undercover work was his life, his calling.

He lifted her chin with his finger and pressed a kiss against her forehead. She stared up into his eyes and envisioned the mixture of gold, brown, and green swirled into one. Slowly his head descended until their lips barely met. She couldn't allow this to happen. Her life didn't have room for romantic involvement and certainly not with a man who lived every moment in the foothills of crisis. She pulled away—not really wanting to, but believing that nestling next to him would spur her heart in a dangerous direction.

"I wouldn't do anything to hurt you," he whispered, toying with a strand of her hair. "You're too important to me."

She hesitated, then leaned back into his embrace, the lure of his kiss too powerful for her to refuse. He lowered his head and gently tasted the lips she timidly offered. His intensity deepened, nearly frightening her, and he released her.

"I should apologize, but I've wanted to kiss you for days."

Before she could respond, headlights flashed behind them, and her father pulled into the parking space beside her car. She eased back to the driver's side and opened the door.

"I'll call you tomorrow," Beau said. "I want to make sure you're okay."

She chose not to respond. Tumultuous emotions caused by his kiss and his intentions to continue with his undercover work frightened her. She wished sleep would dull her senses and bring relief.

"Sorry I'm late," her father said, holding up a plastic container and passing it through the door. "Your mom wanted to make sure Beau had plenty of tonight's soup."

"Thanks," Beau replied, reaching across the car seat to grasp the container. "It'll be gone in no time."

"Come on, Alli," her father said. "Let me walk you up those stairs. Your bodyguard needs time to recuperate."

❧

Beau slept soundly past noon the following day until he woke from the dull ache in his leg. Those stairs at Allison's apartment. A moment later he remembered his trip downtown to see the sarge and admitted he'd overdone it. Great. And he had so many things to accomplish today.

How did the caller get his cell number? Unless one of Beau's informants had turned on him. . . The whole mess could be an inside job, or someone had gone through his trash. The latter was impossible, because he shredded every piece of mail. The conclusion stunk: nothing worse than losing a good informant or a cop going bad. He didn't want to think who it might be.

In the course of considering the past weeks and attempting to put some sense to his case, Beau struggled with the fact that Allison danced across his mind and ruined any good deliberation. From the first moment he saw her, she'd consumed his thoughts, and if he didn't watch it, she'd possess his heart. Last night he'd kissed her, and now guilt riddled him.

He didn't lead women on. Period. In fact, he avoided them. His experiences in the past had been disappointing at best. The women he'd considered had a tendency to wrap their arms around him and beg for him to quit his undercover work. Beau expected God to make it perfectly clear when to find another vocation, and he felt sure it wouldn't come in the form of a woman who didn't understand his need to make the city a better place to live.

But Allison had goals and ambitions of her own. She'd started late in pursuing a nursing career, and her plans were centered on finishing school and paying off the debts incurred to complete her education. She appeared perfectly independent and in no need of a husband. Perhaps a good, solid friendship was in order—one without any threat of the relationship heading into treacherous territory. Like his heart.

Who am I fooling? Allison is perfect for me.

He wanted to spend every spare minute with her, and his defenses were fast losing their resolve. He hated seeing her frightened, especially when this new problem originated with his continuing the case. She'd been through enough with the shooting, and now some thug thought he could get to Beau through a woman. And it worked. That's why he couldn't consider getting involved. Then why did he kiss her? Caution ruled every decision he made, and a woman complicated the ever present danger. Once he nailed the guy threatening her and had him in jail where he belonged, they'd part company. Until then, they could be friends. He simply had to put his heart in check.

Beau glanced at the clock: twelve-thirty. He needed to check in with Sarge about the latest findings and his thoughts about the caller.

He also needed to call Allison—make sure she'd not received anymore phone threats. The climb out of bed to retrieve her number from his pants pocket nearly sent him sprawling to the floor. Grabbing the edge of his nightstand, he steadied himself until he could maneuver. Today would be the pits, but that's what he got for not minding the doctor's or the nurse's advice.

Her phone rang three times before it rolled over to the answering machine. "Hi Allison, this is Beau. Are you there to pick up?"

Her sweet voice sent a tingle to his toes. "Good afternoon. How are you feeling?"

"Like I just got run over by a truck," he said with a chuckle. "You doing all right?"

"Yes, no calls today. I've been wondering, how long before you feel I'm okay to come and go as I please?"

He despised the anxiety in her voice. "You can now, just

not at night. All I want is for you to be careful and let me know where you're going and when you expect to return. Make sure you always have your cell phone with you."

"I see. Life is a little strange when you're always looking over your shoulder."

Beau sighed. "Not when you know who's in control."

"Always the optimist, but I appreciate your attitude."

He glanced around his bedroom. Normally a whole day without demands was a welcome, but not when he hurt and couldn't do all the things he wanted. "Are you busy right now?"

"No. I've cleaned, written out bills, and talked to long lost girlfriends. What did you have in mind?"

"I've got a prescription to fill, and I'm hungry. Are you interested in taxiing around a decrepit old man?"

"Sure." She laughed. "I'd welcome the change of scenery. My apartment is driving me crazy. When do you want to leave?"

"Truthfully, I just woke up. I need to make a few calls and get a shower, which will take a little while with this battered body. How about an hour?" He gave her directions and hung up the phone.

Beau remembered a term his grandmother used to use: tickle. He'd just given himself all the reasons why he shouldn't be anything more than a friend to Allison, and now his heart betrayed him.

Lord, if she is not for me, close the doors. I really like this girl, and despite all the arguments against becoming involved with her, I want to know her more.

❧

Allison laughed until her sides hurt. "If you don't stop, they're going to throw us out of here." She leaned across the restaurant's table in their booth. "You weren't this funny in the hospital."

He bent as though to tell her a secret. "I didn't have this freedom."

She smiled and glanced down at her salad. Refusing to put a damper on their jovial mood, she pushed aside the ugliness that had brought them together. "I didn't think picking up a prescription and heading to lunch would be such entertainment."

"It's the company you're keeping," Beau replied, stabbing a slice of tomato in his salad.

She caught his gaze and saw fire smoldering in those warm eyes. He hastily glanced away. Could he feel as uncomfortable as she about the two of them together?

"Allison," he began and reached for his water glass, "sometimes when two people share a crisis or danger, they're bound forever by a strange magnetic force that other people seldom understand."

"I do understand a little. I've heard my dad talk about the Vietnam War and the special bond of the vets."

"Exactly." He replaced his glass and reached across the table to grasp her hand. "You and I have one of those relationships. We're friends, but with more of a sensitivity than those who experience more good times than bad ones."

"As though woven in a peculiar tapestry?"

"Yes. Part of it is our Christian faith and our certainty of the hereafter. We are more aware of purpose and meaning in our lives."

"Beau, what are you trying to tell me?"

He propped his other elbow on the table and rested his chin on his hand. "I feel I've known you forever. You're driving me crazy. No matter how many times I've tried to logically say you're just a woman with whom I've shared danger,

I find myself thinking about you again, then I'm angry for doing so."

All morning, she'd tried to convince herself she didn't need an undercover policeman in her life. She had a career ahead of her in the field of medicine, one she felt God had ordained for her life. Yet, the attraction for Beau—everything about him—beckoned her.

She shivered, but not from the air conditioning in the restaurant. He stated exactly how she felt. She placed her fork beside the salad, willing the appropriate words to flow from her tongue.

"Strangely enough, I feel the same way. I wish you weren't so likeable—it would make things much easier." She hesitated at the risk of sounding bold. "What do you want to do about us?"

"That's my dilemma. I should pick up my cane, go home, and forget I ever met you, but I can't. This whole thing is not fair to you. You know my line of work and the danger involved."

"Yes, and I respect your commitment."

He rubbed his chin. "I've never had much luck in the romance department."

"Did other women ask you to give up your police work?" She offered a faint smile.

"Exactly. Ultimatums of their so-called love."

"I really understand how a woman could care for you and want to make sure you're safe. From what you've told me, your job is a lonely proposition and involves a lot of hours where no one can contact you. Those circumstances could be difficult."

"How would you feel? I mean. . ." He shifted in the booth. "We've known each other so short a time. But if. . .if we were together, would you be able to handle the stress and pressure?"

Allison stared into his face, knowing she was losing her heart to the man before her. "I don't know, Beau."

ten

"I have to be honest," Allison continued. "Up until a few weeks ago, my life looked pretty ho-hum. Then I was shot by a stranger who thought I was his ex-girlfriend, and now I'm threatened by a guy who believes I'm your girlfriend. Tell me, what would you think?"

Beau's mouth formed a grim line, and he released her hand. He reached into his pocket for his wallet and slapped a twenty dollar bill on the table. "I'll call a taxi for a ride home. You don't need one more minute of this. I don't know what I was thinking."

"No, wait." She reached across the table for his hand. "I said I was being honest, and I'm not finished."

He lifted a brow, but waited with one hand on his cane and the other resting beneath her grasp.

"I don't believe anyone meets by chance, but rather God places people in our lives for a reason. At first, I thought you were there to save my life. Later I wondered if you were to help me through those threats. Now, I honestly don't know. I've told myself repeatedly that you and I have nothing in common, and I'm too busy right now for a man in my life. But. . .my emotions are telling me not to let go."

She saw a flicker of something in his eyes. By his own admission, he wrestled with the same thoughts.

He chewed on his lower lip and glanced down at the hand she'd placed over his. "I should walk away and never bother you again, but I don't want to. Something about you has

.1andcuffed my heart." He offered a faint smile, and she felt her lips tug upward.

Before they could say another word, the server stopped to refill their iced teas.

"Are you staying?" Allison asked, hoping he understood she meant their friendship and not the meal. Odd, she thought she wanted to go back to her own comfortable lifestyle; but when presented with the choice, she changed her mind.

"Some days are tough," he said, neither moving toward his food nor leaning on the cane to stand. "And I've already told you how frustrating my schedule is."

"And dangerous," she added.

"That too. It's probably not a decision to make on the spur of the moment."

"Is that what you're asking?"

He shook his head. "I'd be a fool to force the issue. Like you, I'm confused about us."

"I've seen tough days," she said, wanting him to see she could hold her own in a relationship if necessary.

"Some days, you might not hear from me at all. When you do, I can't tell you where I've been or what I've done."

She nodded. "My dad retired from the navy. He worked Intelligence, and sometimes he was gone for weeks."

He slowly swung his body back to the table and caught her gaze with his. "God has a plan for our lives. Trouble is, He hasn't told me yet if you and I are in it together." He took a long drink of his iced tea. "Whether we decide to continue seeing each other or go our separate ways, I won't discuss this case with anyone but Sarge. Those on both sides of the law have been told I'm on a leave of absence, maybe permanent. I'm still questioning the connection between the shooting and the threats, and there's a lot of investigation to be done."

"I understand. It's scary—all of it."

"So, with that in mind, are we still buds?"

She instantly prayed for guidance. "How about blossoming buds, taking one day at a time?"

❧

An hour later, Allison parked her little blue car in front of Beau's house. Like tin soldiers, three towering pines kept guard of the door, and their stance amused her. When she'd picked him up earlier, he'd been waiting on the driveway for her. She'd assessed his house, thinking the brick two-story looked more like a family home than a single man's domain.

"I know I said this before, but you have a beautiful home and yard. Looks as manicured as a woman's nails."

He laughed. "Thanks. I enjoy gardening and landscaping, but there are times when I have to call on a service to keep it mowed and the weeds pulled," he said. "What saves me are the perennials adding color. The rest is maintenance."

"I've just discovered your hobby," she said, admiring the neatly trimmed shrubbery intermingled with Shasta daisies, hibiscus, which hadn't yet bloomed, pink pentas, golden lantana, Mexican heather, and what her mother called "hummingbird plants."

"Oh, I have another sideline, but you have to come inside to see those projects." He tossed her a grin.

"Are you a man of many talents?" She turned off the engine.

"Not really. My dad tinkered in a bit of everything, and I tagged along, learning a few things along the way."

They exited the car and walked up a winding sidewalk leading to an oak-stained door. As soon as Beau's key turned the lock, the alarm signaled. He hobbled into another room and disarmed it.

She glanced about, impressed by the exquisite, detailed

furniture, some hand-painted and others finished in a rich cherry. She detected the faint scent of a man's citrusy fragrance, a hint of Beau's private realm.

"Gorgeous furniture."

"I like building things," he said simply, "and Dad enjoys painting and staining them."

Her eyes widened. "You built these pieces?" She stepped closer to a small, three-drawer chest that was painted a cream color and trimmed in gold. A green vine stretched across the top and trickled down the sides. "This is lovely. I'm surprised you and your dad haven't gone into the furniture making business."

He shrugged. "We both enjoy it as a hobby, not a vocation. Personally, I don't want people telling me how they want something constructed. Let me show you the bookcases in the den."

She followed him into a kitchen overlooking a sunny breakfast nook and an open TV area. A wall-length, cherry bookcase and entertainment center captured her attention.

"Oh, the scroll work on this is perfect." She noted the mantel above the fireplace held the same wood and scroll design. "I am really impressed." Glancing down at the hardwood floors, she shook her head, knowing the homes in this neighborhood most generally contained carpet. "Did you install the floors too?"

He leaned against the kitchen counter. "Sure did. When my head's spinning about a case, I take to the yard or to the garage. Works like a charm."

Allison saw the perspiration beads mount on his wrinkled forehead. Again he'd overdone it. "Beau, you really should lie down, or you'll be right back in the hospital."

"Aw, Nurse," he said, stuffing his hands into his jeans

pocket and scuffing the toe of his tennis shoe across the floor, imitating a little boy. "I don't wanna much."

"And what did you plan to do instead of take care of the body God gave you?" She folded her arms across her chest in an effort to imitate a stern disciplinarian.

He frowned. "Did you learn that technique in nursing school?"

"No." She laughed. "It's my own."

He eased himself down on a recliner and pointed to a paper grocery sack on the table. "I'd like a nap, but Kieron brought over my mail, and I need to go through it this afternoon and pay bills."

"Nice guy to take care of it for you."

"I feel sorry for him, especially since his wife left him. I keep talking to him about the Lord, but nothing's registered."

"How sad. Do they have children?"

A mass of dark hair fell across his forehead. "No. They were high school sweethearts—never dated anyone else. He caught her running around on him, and when he wanted to make it work, she left." He shook his head. "She never came across to me as the type. Guess I misjudged her."

Not knowing how to reply, Allison decided to head home and hopefully he would rest. "If you don't have any more errands for me, I'm going home," she said with a tilt of her head. "I hope you get some sleep."

"I will think about it," he said without an ounce of commitment.

She sighed and took another quick look around the room. "I have a difficult time picturing you as an undercover cop."

He chuckled and narrowed his eyes. "Do I look mean enough for you now?"

"As compared to what? You don't scare me. Besides, you

look more like a teddy bear." She grinned and groped through her purse for her keys until she tightened her fingers around them. "Thanks for lunch."

"Thanks for hauling me around." He tried to stand, but she protested. "I can at least walk you to the door."

"Another time." She wondered if a daylight kiss would affect her like last night. Feeling herself grow warm, she whirled around for the door and jingled her keys. "Bye. Have a wonderful nap."

She heard him laugh. "I'll call you later."

Once at her car, Allison slid onto the extra warm seat and stuck her key into the ignition. Pressing the air conditioning button, although she knew there wouldn't be any cold air just yet, she paused to take one last glimpse at his house. What a great guy and talented too. Not at all what she envisioned for a man in his line of work. She swung her gaze across the street to where Beau indicated Kieron lived. How sad that his wife had abandoned him. She must remember to pray for the couple.

As her car left the curb, the familiar cloud of gloom settled upon her. For a little while, she'd forgotten the ugliness of what really brought her and Beau together. She prayed the worst had passed, but in the back of her mind a shadow of doubt gripped her.

❧

Beau woke three hours later at the sound of his doorbell. Swinging his legs over the bed, he attempted to stand, but a surge of pain broke huge beads of sweat down the sides of his face. Groaning, he grabbed the cane and limped to the door, wanting to verbally terrorize whoever stood on the opposite side.

Kieron greeted him with a broad smile. "Hey, Beau, how are you feelin'?"

Beau raked his fingers through his hair and forced a greeting he didn't really mean. "Better. Just tired and ready to move on." He stepped back from the door. "Come on in."

"Ah, can't stay but a minute," he said, ducking his head in the doorway. "Just wanted to see how you were doing and if you needed anything."

"No, thanks. Allison stopped over earlier, and we picked up a prescription at the drugstore. Come on in." He leaned on his cane and maneuvered around so Kieron could step inside. His leg hurt something awful after jumping out of bed and putting all of his weight on it. If the stupid thing didn't stop throbbing soon, he'd be under the mercy of another pain pill.

"What about dinner?" Kieron asked. "I could grill us a couple of steaks."

"Allison's mother gave me some soup, and Mom dropped off fried chicken and potato salad. My appetite isn't quite ready to handle a lot of food yet."

"Looks like your pretty little girlfriend is taking good care of you," Kieron said, leaning against the side of the door.

Beau grinned and nodded. "She's a friend, nothing more, but that part of getting better makes it almost worth getting shot."

"So, when are you heading back to work? All those bad guys need you settin' them straight."

"I'm not, at least for a good while. Maybe never. I'm off my current case, and I've taken a ninety-day leave of absence."

Kieron whistled. "That'll be the day when Beau Oliver stuffs his undercover work aside. I bet you intend to stay on cases at home, just not let anybody know."

Beau shook his head. He didn't like lying to people, but Allison's well-being was more important. "The shooting slowed me down. I'm facing rehab three times a week and a pile of projects around here to last all summer. If and when I go back, I don't know what I'll be doing. The way this body of mine looks like a battleground, a desk job sounds good." His last statement held more truth than he cared to admit.

Kieron turned and grasped the doorknob. "You let me know if I can be of help. You certainly were there for me when I cried the blues over Lori leaving."

"No problem. Never know, during this time off, I might finally get you to church."

His friend shook his head. "Don't think so, but I appreciate the offer." He patted his jeans pocket. "I forgot your house key. Do you want me to run it back over?"

"Keep it for now. The way my head has been spinning the last few weeks, I might lock myself out and need it."

"Okay. Get rested up." Kieron turned the knob and let himself out.

Beau didn't waste any time plodding back to bed. A burst of fire-hot pain raced up and down his leg. What did he expect with the doctors removing two bullets in his upper thigh and two more in his stomach? At the moment, pushing a pencil had more appeal than hanging out with the likes of the man who tried to kill him. Allison would agree with him on that observation.

Allison. She'd been honest with him this afternoon, and he respected her candid reply to his question. He'd been lied to enough by women to know the signs. . .first the wheedling into his heart, followed by the poignant remarks of fear and the inevitable crying, and finally the severing of the relationship. Pretense didn't equate to Allison's personality, and although she held the characteristics of a nurse who might tend to smother him, she knew when to give him room. Perhaps God had given him an angel.

He'd rest awhile, call Allison, and tackle the bag of mail. The bottle of pain medication resting on his nightstand alongside a glass of water captured his attention. He knew he needed it; he simply hated to give in. With a sigh, he screwed off the lid and downed a tablet with the water. As his mind grew fuzzy and the pain subsided, he thought about Kieron and how miserable he must feel without the Lord. What Lori had done to him surprised Beau as much as Kieron. She'd always been devoted to him. For certain, Beau didn't intend to give up on his old friends, and he knew the Lord didn't either.

eleven

Beau slumped into his leather recliner and expelled an exhilarating, exhausted sigh. Lethargic, and loving it, he leaned back and launched the footrest into smooth sailing. His leg ached, but he didn't care. Fishing all morning with his dad ranked an inch short of heaven. They'd talked about things from when he was a kid—things he'd nearly forgotten—but once they got started, all those memories rolled fast and furious.

He chuckled. The two hadn't caught a single fish, probably because they hadn't stopped talking long enough for the fish to take a nibble. Beneath a brilliant sunrise and on to the sweltering heat of noon, the sparkling waters lifted his spirits and healed the ache inside him for days gone by. He felt closer to his dad than in years. They'd eaten salami and sharp cheese on rye with gobs of hot mustard, munched on a whole bag of barbecue potato chips, crunched on huge dill pickles, and washed it all down with a gallon of sweetened iced tea. Once they returned home, Mom served a fresh blackberry cobbler and ice cream. What an indulging lifestyle. He could get used to it real fast, even if he had to get himself nearly killed to value the great outdoors and the blessings of terrific parents.

Allison had spent the morning with a girlfriend shopping. They'd both been busy, just apart. She told him yesterday she enjoyed fly fishing and often went with her dad. How could he be so lucky to find such a wonderful woman? He glanced at the phone across the room, wishing it sat right beside him so he could call her without subjecting his bruised body to more torture. He refused to take another pain pill and waste the rest of the day sleeping.

"I'm getting old," he told himself. "Can't even dodge speeding bullets anymore." No wonder they hadn't hooked any fish this morning.

His own thoughts caught up with him. A couple of matters had cropped up since he'd found more time to think about his old case, the shooting, and the phone threats. The phone. . . Attributing his suspicions to his wary mind or preferably his moxie, he wondered if his house could be bugged. Sarge would most likely get a hoot out of this one, so he'd keep his ungrounded suspicions to himself. No one knew where he lived. . .but how else would someone know he'd almost figured out who stood behind the narcotics ring?

Since he'd decided to continue with the case, he'd keep his deliberations to himself and make his calls away from home until he purchased a new cell phone. Beau shook his head. He was either getting smarter or senile. Time would tell.

Forcing himself from the easy chair, he limped across the room to the cell phone. He turned it over in his hands and slid out the plastic flap housing the battery. Nothing out of the ordinary there. He took a moment to study the handset before disassembling it. After finding it perfectly intact, he laughed at himself and put it back together. Good thing he hadn't mentioned this aspect of the case to Sarge. He'd have ordered a psychological workup.

Maneuvering back to his easy chair, he punched in Allison's number while glancing at his watch: two o'clock. A smile tugged at his mouth as he anticipated the mellifluous sound of her voice.

"Hi, this is Allison. I'm not at home right now, but if you'll leave a message, I'll get right back with you."

"Hey, Nurse Allison, this is your decrepit bodyguard. Give me—"

"Good afternoon," she said, and he envisioned her sea green eyes dancing with an impish twinkle. "Are you laden down with fish?"

"Not exactly." He laughed and went on to explain the glorious hours with his dad. "And did you buy out the mall?"

"Oh, I found a shoe sale, but I limited myself to one pair of totally awesome, comfortable sandals. My budget wouldn't allow any more."

"How's your budget on gas?" he asked, once again leaning back in his recliner.

"Full tank, all ready for work on Monday morning."

He didn't want to convey his worries about her heading back to the Budget Builder. God could handle his apprehensions much better. "Do you think you might consider transporting a gnarled old man to the grocery?"

"Gnarled?" she laughed. "My amiable side would consider it a worthy cause—you know, help the needy."

"I definitely fall under the title of 'needy.' I'd like to take you to dinner and possibly a movie for your trouble, if you don't already have plans."

"Hmm, Officer Oliver, you drive a hard bargain. How about if I cook dinner and we rent a movie? You're recuperating, or have you forgotten?"

He frowned and let out a feigned sigh. "My first weekend home, and you want me to resign myself to taking it easy. Unfortunately, I'm at your mercy."

"You have a deal."

"I need to shower and wash off the smell of sweat and the lake. Wouldn't want to scare away my taxi driver."

She laughed, and he thought how much he missed her.

"Everything quiet today?"

Silence pelted his senses. Finally she answered. "No problems, and I'm obeying you and Sergeant Landow."

"Good girl," he whispered. "Soon it will all be over."

They agreed on a time, and he limped from his chair to the shower. Odd, how he suddenly found more energy in knowing he'd see Allison soon.

At the grocery, she teased him unmercifully about squeezing the tomatoes and picking through a whole bin of purple onions for just the right one to make his prize-winning roast and potatoes.

"Now that I'm home, I might as well be a gourmet chef," he said, holding up an onion to the light. "By the way, I'm cooking tonight."

"I don't think so," she replied, examining two good-sized potatoes and placing them in the cart.

"I asked to take you to dinner, not for you to wait hand and foot on me. I might be a bit slow on my feet, but I'm still a prideful man." He attempted to scowl but couldn't hold the pose.

"Okay, let's make a deal," she said. "You sit on your patio and grill the chicken breasts while I bake the potatoes, make a salad, and throw together something for dessert."

"I hear a 'not fair' in all that."

She shrugged and gave him a flirty smile. "Of course it's a fair deal. I simply don't want my chicken burned."

He grabbed a loaf of the grocery's fresh, hot bread and inhaled deeply, allowing its delectable aroma to drive him to distraction while Allison picked through plump, juicy strawberries. For a moment, he felt guilty about refusing Kieron's offer for dinner the night before.

En route to the dairy aisle for whipped cream, Beau found himself face to face with Lori Bates—a very pregnant Lori Bates.

"Hi Beau," she said with a fragile smile. "I haven't seen you in months."

Who's fault is that, since you walked out on Kieron? He didn't want to debate her obvious infidelity. "Been busy, working."

"I'd heard you'd been hurt. Are you mending okay?"

"Sure. I'll be running in no time at all. I'd like you to meet somebody." He turned to Allison and introduced the two women.

Lori's hand covered her protruding stomach, and her gaze flitted about the dairy section, then back to him. "I'm sorry I didn't talk to you before I left. Frankly, I didn't know if you could help or not."

"I wish you had," he replied, thinking about how Kieron had cried for weeks about his wife. "Maybe I could have helped—recommended counseling or something."

"It may not be too late," she said wistfully. "I miss Kieron, but the baby's welfare is more important."

Confused, Beau waited for her to say more.

"You don't know what I'm talking about, do you?" She continued to look uneasy.

He shook his head. "Not really." Kieron wouldn't hurt her or a baby, even if the child didn't belong to him.

Her eyes pooled with tears, and she brushed back a strand of auburn hair. "He's addicted to cocaine," she whispered. "I discovered it months before I moved out, although I suspected the abuse for a long time. When I found out about the baby and Kieron still refused to get help, I had no choice but to move out. Wishful thinking, I guess, but I hoped he loved me and the baby enough to leave it alone."

"What? Kieron, a user?" Beau asked, his heart pounding like a sledgehammer. "There's got to be a mistake."

She shook her head. "No, it's true. Kieron never came near you when he was high. I assumed he feared with your line of work and all, you'd catch on in a heartbeat."

A million thoughts raced through Beau's mind. Never, not ever, had he detected drug abuse from Kieron. In fact, he doubted it now.

"I can only imagine what he told you about my leaving," Lori said. "I phone him regularly, but he either hangs up or doesn't return my calls. As his friend, perhaps you can stop in unexpectedly. He has a lot of respect for you, and I know he'd listen." She reached into her purse and ripped off a square of paper from a notebook and jotted down something. "Here are my home and work phone numbers. I'm with my parents until I can get on my feet. I. . .I am attending church again." She glanced around him to Allison. "Nice to meet you, Allison. You have a great guy here."

She pushed her cart past them while Beau fumbled through his recollections of all Kieron had told him about finding Lori with another man, all those sordid facts that Beau didn't want to hear at the time, but his friend had needed to tell him. Kieron had spent hours with Beau, shedding buckets of tears over his high school sweetheart, the love of his life.

Beau turned to Allison, the revulsion for Lori Bates causing him to tremble. "I don't believe a word of it," he muttered. "Kieron may have bent the law in his younger days, just like I did, but he'd never lower himself to the degradation of drugs." He clenched his fists. "I'm a cop. I'd have seen it in his eyes, and he knows how I feel about users and pushers. Lori must think I'm a complete fool."

Allison shrugged. "Even if Kieron hid it from you? Even if he's so addicted that he couldn't quit?"

He swung his gaze at her, then to Lori pushing her cart away down the aisle. "Impossible. I know the classic signs. He's clean. She should have realized I'd see through her story."

Allison reached into the dairy case and pulled out a carton of whipped cream. Her lips pressed firmly together, and her silence spoke volumes about her impression of Lori Bates.

"You believe her, don't you?" Irritation rippled up his spine.

Allison paused, her doubts vivid in a faint smile. "I don't know either of them, Beau. They're your friends, and I'm an outsider. But I can't help wondering which one is telling the truth."

twelve

Allison felt Beau's hand slip over hers as the choir sang a final refrain to Sunday's special music. As the organ completed its portion, the melodious harmony touched her soul with the peace she so desperately needed. How refreshing to spend this morning at Beau's church! She'd accompanied him when he mentioned driving himself to the worship service—a feat he didn't need to attempt just yet. She admired his church, the expanse of oak evident in the many rows of pews, the stairways curving up to the balcony, and detailed trim. The deep green carpet gave the illusion of walking in a thick forest. Definitely a beautiful sanctuary.

She focused on the cross behind the choir loft and considered how she depended on Jesus to get her through each day. The threats had stopped, but the fear remained, and the idea of being followed made her nauseous. What if the caller continued to spy on her as he'd done before? Beau said she could relax, but his reassurance didn't help the uneasiness or queasiness. She believed he knew more than he admitted about the case, but he wasn't offering any information, and she didn't know what specific questions to ask.

Deep in the recesses of her heart, she thought all the happenings of this last month were connected, but where did all the pieces fit? Repeatedly, she wondered if she'd seen or heard something illegal at the Budget Builder. Nothing flashed across her mind, while frustration and terror twisted at her heart.

Beau wasn't invincible; the shooting proved his vulnerability. He could tease and refer to himself as her bodyguard, but the unseen enemy had already dealt a nasty blow. God, and God alone, held their destiny.

Destiny. She wondered if this fragile thread of love tying her heart to Beau's would be strong enough to keep them together. She fully understood how a woman could abandon a relationship with him. The ever present danger easily provided a multitude of sleepless nights. Yet, if Beau's undercover work resulted from God's plan, he must continue, for being out of His will meant a spiritual death more tragic than anything man could do.

She had agreed to deepen their friendship, fully aware of the hazards and equally unable to say no. Whatever the reasons for them being together, she intended to stay until God guided them apart.

Beau squeezed her hand, and she realized she trembled in the wake of her own thoughts. He knew what assaulted her ponderings, although they didn't speak of it. If she stared into his hazel eyes, he might see her honest uncertainties. He lived in a different world from hers, and as much as she wanted to be there, the thought petrified her.

"Thanks for the taxi service," he whispered. "I like having you sit next to me."

She could feel him studying her. "You're welcome, and I like being here too."

"We've come a long way in such a short time," he went on. "Don't be afraid."

"But I am," she replied, keeping her attention fixed on the choir. "I want to be this tower of strength, but I'm not."

"Do you want to call it quits? It might be easier if we weren't together."

She stiffened. "No. That's the crazy part. I want to be right here beside you."

ஃ

Beau felt Allison's clammy hand firmly within his grasp. Was he fooling himself? With all of his thoughts and prayers heading skyward for God to shelter his angel, had he self-ishly overlooked the real problem? In his desire to protect her, had he put her into a more perilous position? Would the joker truly not harass her anymore? Questions and more questions, all without answers. Each time he gave the matter to God, he yanked it back and tried to tell Him how to go about His business. How unlike a Christian. *How like me.*

In his undercover work, he played with people's minds. He lived among the bad guys, talked their talk, did what they did, got arrested with them, deceived whomever he could, and then looked for the big opportunities to throw them in jail. Granted, he had a calling and a ministry, but too often he didn't feel any better than the guys he arrested. Sometimes he felt like an actor on stage instead of a lowly man bent on cleaning up the streets from drug dealers and users. There were times when the tacky clothes, the trashed-out cars, and those he associated with made him question if he was any better than those he exposed.

He believed God knew his heart, but sometimes Beau doubted himself. He thrived on the adrenaline rush and excitement surrounding his work. The thrill of danger put him into deeper and more dangerous situations. Had it all moved from God's ministry to Beau's private entertainment center? He hoped not; he prayed not.

In thinking about Allison and how his heart had taken a huge plunge, he once again considered a desk job. Other undercover cops were just as good, most of them better, but they didn't know the Lord. They didn't pray over the young and old roaming the streets in search of a fast buck or a way to escape their depressing worlds. He did, and often while talking with them.

Am I in Your will, Lord? Am I being a humble servant, or have I gravitated to becoming a self-seeker? Oh, Father, I pray my motives are pure. I don't want to wake up one morning and despise myself. Please, Lord, protect my Allison. If it means letting her go, then I will. I want to be obedient.

Beau knew her life and his rested in the Father's hands. He pushed aside his apprehensions and turned his attention to the pastor and worshipping the Lord.

❧

On Monday morning, Allison collected her courage and arrived at the Budget Builder ten minutes before it opened. The extra time provided an opportunity to pray before taking the leap from her car to the employees' entrance.

She anticipated curious and often insensitive onlookers would hurl questions like a rock avalanche, and she didn't particularly want to relive the shooting for the sake of lacing someone's mind with gory details. In fact, she'd like to wear a sign saying "Don't ask, 'cause I don't want to talk about it." Although that attitude best described her feelings, it sounded a bit immature.

Lord, help me to be sweet to everyone, not only the ones who are sincere and mean well, but also those who have a tendency to glorify crime.

Allison took a deep breath and opened the car door. The security guard stood by the entrance, but his presence didn't alleviate her anxiety. His presence didn't help one bit the morning of the shooting. Only God gave her peace of mind.

Soon her fears diminished and, for the most part, she easily swung back into her old routine. Even her friend, Mr. Billings, stopped in a little after seven o'clock.

"Hey, Sunshine. Good to see you," he said with his familiar smile. "I prayed for you and the people involved in that nasty business. How is the man who tried to help you?"

"Thanks. He's home from the hospital," she replied, appreciating his discretion. She glanced about them. "This is my first day back, and I'm a little nervous."

Mr. Billings grasped the plastic Budget Builder's bag and leaned over the counter. "Before you know it, that business will be behind you, like a pesky nightmare. Me and the missus pray for you regularly."

She watched him stride away, thinking how much she'd miss his charm and encouragement once she completed her education.

At noon, she munched on a turkey sandwich and soda in the employees' break room. Allison talked freely with two women, but they seemed uncomfortable. Finally, the situation had grated at her nerves long enough.

"Okay, what's the problem? You two act like I have the plague."

The older woman, near her mother's age, cleared her throat. "We're not sure what to say, Allison. You went through a terrible ordeal, and we're both afraid of saying the wrong thing and upsetting you."

Heaviness rested on Allison's shoulders. "Look, I'm still me. Nothing's changed for you to act differently. I had a horrible experience, and it's over. The idea of talking about it turns my stomach, but we had plenty to talk about before the shooting. Please, relax and be my friends again."

The older woman pulled a sleeve of crackers from her lunch sack. "Deal," she said, "and since I'm the mama here,

I'll spread the word."

Allison gave her and the younger African American woman a hug. She noticed her friend's lunch. "Tricia, did your mom make a strawberry pie?"

Tricia beamed. "Yeah, and there's enough for you, Mama Grayson, and me."

Once they finished dessert and chatted about the store, Mrs. Grayson and Tricia decided to take a stroll outside before heading back to work. Allison picked up her cell phone and punched in Beau's number. She knew he had rehab scheduled for late morning, but she wanted to leave a message. She laughed at his greeting.

"Hey, this is Beau. Not here. Gone fishing. Throw me a line, and I'll hook up with you when I get back."

"Hi, this is Allison. I wanted to tell you that work has been just fine, and my jitters have nearly vanished. Hope the therapist hasn't overworked you today."

Allison headed back to work, and for the first time she felt like nothing had ever happened. Later in the afternoon, she heard someone call her name, looked up, and saw Kieron in her cashier's line. She smiled and waved, but a huge lump settled in the bottom of her stomach. Ever since she'd met his wife at the grocery and listened to her conversation with Beau, something about the man bothered her. Normally she didn't prejudge a person, but to be blunt, Kieron Bates made her skin crawl.

Lord, help me. I'm not thinking Christlike thoughts here. Kieron is Beau's friend, and he should know his friend better than I.

"Kieron is a great guy," Beau had said. "I don't know what I would have done without him while I was stuck in the hospital."

By the time she checked out three customers ahead of Kieron, she'd convinced herself that she'd misjudged him.

"How are you doing?" she asked as he handed her a bag of roofing nails. His fingers wrapped around her hand, but she pretended not to notice and pulled back.

"Great. Even better now that I have you ringing me up," he said low.

"Seen your neighbor today?" *Is it me, or is Kieron coming on to me?*

"Naw. I left at the crack of dawn. Doubt if he was stirring then." He produced a credit card, and she swiped it through a machine beside her register.

Feeling his gaze upon her, she glanced up. His violet eyes met hers with a lusty sheen, and it angered her.

"Want to take in a movie tonight?" he asked huskily.

"No, thanks."

"Why? Got plans?"

"Yes, with Beau." *The nerve of him.*

"Cancel them. I can show you a better time. I'll throw in dinner at a nice place and anything else you want."

She paused, forming the right words to let him know exactly what she thought of his crude behavior. "I'm not interested," she replied, "not now or ever."

"Aw, aren't you tired of the cop yet?"

She glared straight into Kieron's eyes. Disgust raced through her body. "I wonder what he'd think of this conversation, especially coming from his best friend."

Kieron chuckled. "He wouldn't believe you. I'm his bud."

"Don't be too sure of that."

She tore off the signature portion of the register slip and set it on the counter with a pen. He scribbled his name and grabbed his bag.

"I bet you're a great kisser," he said for only her ears. "I'll find out soon enough."

Allison crossed her arms. "I don't think so."

"I'm only teasing," he said with a grin that unnerved her. "No hard feelings?"

"Of course not." *I'll just consider the source.*

thirteen

Beau limped into the waiting room to inform his dad he'd been released from rehab jail. The session had been gruesome, and he ached all over. After complaining to the male therapist during the entire hour with no results, Beau wanted to tear apart something or someone in retaliation. Instead, he pasted on a smile, realizing his dad didn't need to face a surly son.

"Ready for lunch?" Beau asked, while pain washed over his body.

"Of course. Were they hard on you in there?"

Beau gritted his teeth. "Like a torture chamber."

His dad chuckled. "I can tell by the look on your face. What about some red-hot chili to add a little color?"

"And add indigestion to my whipped body?" He shrugged. "Why not? Gotta get this man back into shape."

At the restaurant, he decided to check his messages at home and give Sarge a call from the pay phone. He still suspected someone had leaked vital police information, and the thought lingered like a dull headache. Right now, Beau's head pounded. He swallowed two headache tablets and gave the waitress his order for chili with a side of jalapenos.

He punched in his number and listened to Allison's angelic voice leave an upbeat message about her first day back at work. Grinning like a kid, he phoned her home number.

"Hey, Angel, glad your first day is a success. I know I'm whining, but this rehab is going to make an old man out of me. I'll call you later."

Before contacting Sarge, he studied the area about him—a

habit he didn't feel safe to give up. His boss answered on the second ring.

"Sarge, just checking in. Can you tell me who's working with Ace on my case?"

"GW. I believe you've worked with him a few times."

"Yeah, great guy. Both of them are looking at spending a lot of days hanging out with those guys. It took me months to build up their trust, and even when I bought a couple of pounds of dope, I never found out who was supplying." He hesitated. "I take that back. I must have stumbled onto something because of the threats Allison and I received."

"Any new developments?

"Not a thing I can pass on," Beau replied. "The street's pretty quiet."

"You be careful, and call me day or night when you put it all together. You're the best I've got Beau, and I'm counting on you."

"Not much pressure there," Beau said. "You'll be the first to know, which brings me to another matter. Until I get a new cell, don't call me at home or on my other cell phone."

Sarge chuckled. "Suspicious, are you? Probably a good idea, since we don't know where the leak is."

"And I'm becoming more and more convinced that the shooting and my case are linked. I still need a few more pieces. I'd like more info on the gunman: any family members involved with the police, including his wife, who else lived in his apartment complex, and if Lopez had any other arrests. Put the word out on the streets, and keep me posted."

Beau replaced the receiver and joined his dad. The waitress had set steamy bowls of chili before them along with generous slices of jalapeno cornbread plus an additional bowl of jalapenos. His dad wasted no time in blessing their lunch and digging in.

"Your mother would have a fit if she knew I was eating

this," his dad said with a grin and lifted the spoon to his lips. "Of course, I'll have a hard time explaining the heartburn."

"We'll get some antacid before going home," Beau replied, thinking he'd need some too. One disadvantage of working undercover was that the greasy, spicy food had a habit of coming back to haunt him.

His dad rubbed his nose, a prerequisite to whatever he planned to say. "We—your mom and I—really like Allison."

"Good," Beau replied, taking a generous bite of the cornbread.

"Uh, is there anything else in the making?" He rubbed his nose again and reached for his soupspoon.

"Like what?" Beau asked, inwardly amused. "Oh, you mean are Allison and I seeing each other?"

His dad reached for his glass of water. "You could make this a little easier for your old man."

"And spoil the fun?" Beau took a generous bite of the chili and let it slide down his throat before replying. He pointed his spoon at his dad. "If anyone else asked me about Allison, I'd say we're just friends, and don't be repeating what I'm going to say, especially to Mom—at least not yet. But I like Allison. She's intelligent, strong, independent, drop-dead gorgeous, honest, and a pretty good cook. On top of that, she doesn't smother me, speaks her mind—in fact, I like the way she strings her thoughts together—and most importantly, she's a Christian."

His dad tilted his head back and laughed. "Is there anything about her you don't like?"

Beau joined him. "Not yet." The fact that she questioned Kieron's story about Lori bothered him a little, but not enough to dissuade him. After all, she spoke her mind, and he didn't want a woman to always agree with him, just sometimes.

"I think you have a winner there," his dad said.

"And I think you're right."

Later on that evening, he called Allison at home to hear more about her day.

"Some of the employees didn't know what to say to me at first," she said. "But by the close of the shift, it was like I hadn't been gone."

"Good. I don't want my girl overdoing it. What hours do you work during school?"

"Depends on which hospital I do my clinical rotation at."

Beau detected something amiss in her voice. "Is there anything wrong?"

Silence.

"Alli?"

She expelled a heavy sigh. "Kieron came into the store this afternoon. He asked me out, Beau, and he didn't mince words about it either."

Beau chuckled. "I'm sure he was teasing. You just need to get to know him."

"No, thanks. I have better things to do." Agitation edged her words.

"I'm sorry you're upset," he said, once more regretting Allison's view of his friend. "I'll speak to him about it, and I'm sure he'll apologize."

"No, leave the matter alone. I'll deal with him myself. I'm a big girl."

Her words stung. "I know you can take care of yourself, but he insulted you, which means I'm involved."

"Beau, the last thing I want to do is come between friends. Just forget about it unless it happens again."

"Are you sure?" Somehow he didn't believe her.

"Yes. And you're right: I don't know Kieron. I probably misinterpreted what he said."

But he didn't believe her for a moment.

❧

"I can't believe I'm spending my day off helping you pull

weeds," Allison moaned, wiping the perspiration dripping from her nose. "I've worked six days a week for three weeks straight. I should be resting or stretching out by the pool at my apartment."

"Oh, but you look so adorable with dirt sprinkled across your cheeks," Beau said. "And hard work is good for the soul."

She stood and feigned exasperation. "Show me the chapter and verse."

"Oh, it's in there. I think Genesis. . .something about the sweat of your brow."

She picked up the hose and aimed it in his direction. "This lady packs a thirty-eight," she said, scrunching her eyes in an effort to look tough.

"Won't work. That's a fifty-foot hose, not a thirty-eight." He eased closer, tossing her a huge grin. "You don't want to use that on me."

"Watch it, Fella. I've been out in this heat for three hours. The ice in the water has melted, along with my makeup, and you said we were going to plant flowers—not pull weeds. Besides, you promised lunch, which means I'm hot, tired, thirsty, hungry, and grouchy, and that means you're in trouble."

"I'm going to take good care of you. We're merely clearing the way for those zinnias and marigolds," he said gently.

"Right. I think you got yourself some free labor. Besides, those flowers are annuals not perennials."

He tilted his head and stepped closer. "Thought since I had time on my hands at home, I'd add a little color to the beds." He clamped his foot down on the hose.

Allison pressed on the nozzle handle, but only a dribble of water made its way to the ground. "You cheated," she cried.

"Don't mess with a cop," he whispered. "We have our ways—secret, cunning, and definitely clever." He reached for the hose.

"Not so fast." She jerked her hand from his grasp, no

longer able to control her laughter. "I've watched a few police shows in my time, and you're a leg short of being as fast as I am."

Worry lines creased his forehead. "Are you taking advantage of a wounded man? A man who risked his life for you?"

"Absolutely." She wished she could see his eyes, but his sunglasses stopped her.

He groaned, and his injured leg buckled beneath him. She dropped the hose and rushed to his aid. Instantly he snatched up the nozzle and turned it on her, full blast. Water showered her from head to toe, but it felt wonderful.

"How could you do that to me?" she screamed, using her hands to shield her face. "Me, a defenseless female."

She took off running, realizing his leg would slow him.

"You can run, but you can't hide," he called after her, as she raced down the driveway. She remembered another hose at the rear of the house and quickly turned on the water. Snatching up the nozzle, she met him in the driveway—armed and dangerous. She sprayed him unmercifully, despite his protests, but he returned her fire with vigor. Every inch of her dripped.

"Okay, I give," she finally said, holding her aching side as she laughed.

"Oh, but you gave a great fight," he said in between his own laughter. He dropped his hose and headed her way wearing the look of a properly chided little boy. "My poor baby is soaking wet," he said. "I think she needs someone to hold her."

"Don't you pull that sweet stuff on me." She held him back with an outstretched arm. "I'm on to your games."

He slipped off his sunglasses. "See, I'm truly sorry."

"Then, get me a towel so I can dry off and head home."

"But we were going to have lunch." His sad voice melted her resolve to find a way to get even.

"I'll bring some back. We can finish pulling weeds and

plant your flowers this afternoon."

After he produced a towel, she borrowed it to sit on for the ride home. No matter she looked a sight, she'd had fun, but they always did.

Over an hour later, she pulled up in front of his house with a deli bag full of sandwiches, chips, and drinks. He'd finished the weeding, and some of the flowers filled in the bare spots. The added color did look good.

She smiled. Like a little boy, he couldn't wait to get started on his project. Snatching up her purse and the food bag, she exited her car and spotted what her dad called a junk car parked on the other side of Beau's driveway. The vehicle hadn't been there when she left. It must belong to a neighbor kid. She made her way up the sidewalk to Beau's front door and pressed the doorbell. The sound of deep laughter rose from inside his house. He must have company. Perhaps she should have phoned first. Too late—Beau opened the door.

"Hi," he greeted, "come on in." He took the bag. "Hmm, this smells great, and I'm starved. I've got some friends I'd like for you to meet."

Feeling like she just walked into a male bonding project, Allison started to protest, but he insisted.

"These guys have heard all about you," he said and motioned her inside.

She allowed him to usher her to the kitchen. Three of the worst characters she'd ever seen sat around his kitchen table drinking sodas. One wore an orange bandana tied around his head, two earrings, a white, sleeveless T-shirt, and jeans with a huge hole at the knee. To top it off, he sported a three-day-old beard. Another had bleached blond hair longer than hers and looked just as grimy as the first. The third man, an African American fellow with a huge, round face, didn't have a hair on his shiny head and was dressed in black. He wore more earrings on one ear than she owned. These were Beau's friends! She swallowed hard and managed a fragile smile.

"Guys, this is Allison." They all raised their hands and waved. He pointed to the earring man. "That's Ace. Orange bandana-man is Freddie, and blondie is GW."

"I think I might get myself all shot up for a girl as pretty as you," Freddie commented.

"Yeah, me too," GW said. "You always get all the breaks, Beau—long vacations, someone to bring you lunch, and you were always the first one out of jail."

Beau laughed and turned to her. "It's okay, really. You can relax. These guys work undercover with me."

Allison felt as though someone had lifted a ton of bricks from her shoulders. "I see," she said and glanced from one of his friends to the other. Did Beau look like this when he worked? She remembered his offensive T-shirt. "Well, you certainly had me fooled."

Freddie chuckled. "One look at your face was enough to shake the devil. Has Beau ever told you about his exploits as Superman?"

She stared at him blankly, not sure if she wanted to hear or not.

"Don't believe a word," Beau replied. "They haven't slept since yesterday, and they're punchy."

Ace finished his soda and set the can on the table. "Normally, we're sleeping now, but we had big business this morning. Then, Freddie here thought it would be a good idea to see Superman. There he was, sitting in the grass planting flowers. Wish I'd had my camera."

"I'm glad you came by, even if you saw me taking life easy," Beau said. "Want another soda?"

"No thanks," Ace said. "We've got to get home. Besides, the lady brought you lunch."

The three rose from the table and made their way to the back door.

"Good to meet you," Ace called, and the other two men echoed him. After a few minutes of tossing barbs back and forth with Beau, they left.

He closed the door and hobbled back into the kitchen. Wrapping his arms around her, he grinned. "The look on your face was priceless. I should have called to warn you, so I apologize for that—and for drowning you earlier."

She hesitated. So many things about him surprised her. "You're forgiven." She played with the collar of his clean shirt and asked wistfully, "Superman, huh? Will I ever really know Beau Oliver, undercover cop, gardener, friend, and bodyguard?"

He drew her to him tighter and hugged her close. "I'm not complex. Time is all it takes." He cupped her chin and planted a light kiss on her lips. "I'd spill my guts to you for a sandwich and some chips."

"I should have brought steak. Bet I could have learned a world of things about Superman's wildest adventures."

"I don't think you'd recognize me in action," he whispered, nuzzling her neck. "Sometimes I look pretty bad."

An image of Ace, GW, and Freddie rose in her mind. She had a choice of her old, quiet, comfortable life—or marching on with Beau. With a sigh, she leaned against his chest. No matter the outcome, this was where she wanted to be.

She swallowed her emotion. "I remember back in May when a local Christian radio station hosted a month-long prayer vigil for National Policeman Month."

"Yes, and the station distributed blue bracelets engraved with the names of officers to remind the wearer to pray for them."

She nodded. "I had one of those bracelets, and at the end of that month I stuck mine in my prayer journal so I'd continue praying. At the time, I didn't know any officers personally, other than a few acquaintances at church. Now I see the real sacrifice necessary for those who choose to protect and serve our city. I know I'll never look at an officer again without appreciating his commitment, or," and she smiled, "wondering if some strange character is really working undercover."

fourteen

Beau limped to a pay phone at the grocery store. After he'd spent another morning in his yard, his leg had begun to ache. He wondered if it would ever be back to normal. The therapist said yes, but Beau's patience ran thin with the prognosis. He'd run five miles a day before the shooting, and now he couldn't stand on it for very long without a burst of fire racing up and down his body.

I should be glad I'm alive, he told himself. *Thank You, Lord. Sometimes I lose track of all the blessings You've given me.*

His mind lingered on Allison—her face, her smile, her delightful perspective on things, that mischievous sparkle in her eyes when she teased him. Guess his dad had been right. He had it bad. Beau wanted to tell her he loved her, but not yet. His confession could scare her away. First things first, which meant nailing the guy who threatened her. With no evidence to prove his gut feeling, he knew the shooting and the threats were part of the same scheme.

He glanced about and picked up the phone outside the store, punching in Sarge's number.

"Hey, the fellas stopped by to see me around noon. Said they had an earlier meeting with you, but that's all. I know they believe I'm off the case and didn't want to tell me more."

"Right. Seems like they get one lousy lead after another. They've made some buys but can't get enough trust to make a bigger one."

"My informant says our man is close to home," Beau said.

"So, you're still thinking it's from the inside?"

"I'm leaning in that direction. I know the cops on my list all checked out—and don't say a word about the fellas working on the case. I've known them for a lot of years."

"Beau, it could be anybody, and the person we're looking for is probably the last one any of us would suspect."

He raked his fingers through his hair. Freddie, Ace, and GW's faces and their commitment stood foremost in his thoughts. The idea one of them might be behind the calls churned his stomach. They'd been in some tight places together, and he refused to even consider them.

"I'll keep digging," Beau said.

"Keep in touch."

He hung up the phone and started for his car when his pager sounded. Exhaling a heavy breath, he saw the callback number came from Ace. Retracing his steps, he contacted his old friend. They'd worked together for seven years.

"Beau," Ace began. "I didn't want to tell you this in front of GW and Freddie, but I heard you found out too much when you were working the streets."

"Yeah, I heard the same thing. Sure wish I knew what it was. I've racked my brain trying to find out. Yet, nothing."

"Be careful, okay? Lately Superman hasn't done too good in dodging bullets. I know you're into religion and all, so light a candle or whatever it is you do."

"I pray, Ace." Beau chuckled. "And I appreciate your concern. How about sitting down and talking about Jesus sometime?"

"Not today, but one day soon. I promise."

❧

Frustrated, Beau kicked the right rear tire of his truck, the one slashed identical to the left rear tire. That's what he got for leaving his vehicle parked on the driveway last night instead of putting it in the garage. He'd talked to Alli on the phone until after midnight, then rolled over and went to sleep. Laziness. Pure laziness had caused this.

Beau walked to the end of the driveway. Frustration riddled his senses. He scanned the houses up and down his street. While his neighbors took their safety for granted, he and other fellow police officers risked their lives to keep them secure.

Possibly those foiling his case could have initiated the tire slashing to let Beau know they lurked in the shadows. The suspicion brought a nasty taste to his mouth. Never, absolutely never, had a case plagued him so. While he played cat-and-mouse with these guys, more drug deals went down, and Allison lived in constant fear. Oh, she didn't admit it, but he knew the truth. She thought she masked her trepidation, but her eyes told it all.

I live and breathe undercover. First these guys get my phone numbers and now they have my address. Last night was just their way of letting me know my cover's blown. Well, I take that personal, real personal. I wasn't being paranoid when I wondered if my place is bugged—they really do know where I live.

Palming his fist into his other hand, Beau ambled back up the driveway. What a great way to start a day. He dreaded calling Allison. Last week, she spent her day off helping him weed his flowerbeds, and in recompense he wanted to take her to the beach today. He glanced at his watch; he was supposed to pick her up in fifteen minutes. Some boyfriend he turned out to be. Now, he had to cancel their plans of spending the day in Galveston.

&

Allison tossed her beach bag into the trunk of her car. Poor Beau. He sounded so pitiful in explaining what happened to his truck—pitiful and angry. She couldn't blame him. Probably kids, he'd said, but she wondered if it was a stunt from the man who insisted upon making their lives miserable.

"I'm sorry, Alli," he'd said. "I wanted you to have this great day at the beach, but now we're stuck here."

"No, we're not," she'd replied, determination taking over. "We can take my car."

"Absolutely not. You've hauled me around long enough. I'll see about renting a truck."

"Don't argue with me," she said pointedly. "Besides, I'm on my way, and you can drive my car if it makes you feel any better. I'm not letting a little matter about whose vehicle we take stop our plans. Just go ahead and call the towing service to get your truck taken care of, and I'll be there before you know it." She hung up before he could spout all his arguments that indicated his pride had been damaged.

Thirty minutes later, Beau drove south on I-45 en route to Galveston. The day promised to be glorious, not a cloud in the sky, and Allison imagined a balmy breeze blowing in off the ocean and the rhythmic lull of the waves crashing against the shore. She'd tucked stale bread inside her bag to feed the seagulls, along with plenty of sunscreen—more for Beau than herself.

"You have a nice car," Beau said, sounding as though he'd dealt with not driving his truck. "Handles well."

"Thank you. Dad found it for me when I entered nursing school and needed something reliable."

"When did you get interested in nursing?" He turned down the volume on the car stereo.

"I suppose I was born with this need to care for hurting people. Right from the start, I bandaged my dolls, my brothers, and my sisters—anything that would hold still long enough for me to play nurse." She flashed him a smile. "Note, I said care, not smother."

He grinned and nodded. "Point well taken."

"We moved a lot with Dad in the navy, and I tended to be shy, so my friends were my patched-up dolls."

"Sounds rather sad." He envisioned a lonely little girl with her family of bandage-covered dolls. "I would have thought you played with all your brothers and sisters."

She laughed. "I'm the youngest, remember? And a whiny, spoiled pain. They usually hid from me."

"A brat? You?"

"Exactly." But she wanted to punch him. "In fact my childish attitude is why I'm late in completing my education. I played all during junior high and high school, thinking if God intended for me to be a nurse, then He'd give me the willingness to study. Obviously, my excuse didn't work."

"Ouch! Learned things the hard way, huh? Well, I'm proud of you, and I know you'll be a perfect nurse. Look how well you've taken care of me. I've never felt a single shot—they all felt like kisses."

"Charmer," she accused and laughed with him.

"Where are you headed with your career? Pediatrics? Working in a doctor's office?"

She tilted her head and tried to picture his response. "Inner city hospital. I want my faith and my nursing skills to make a difference."

He raised a brow. "Wow, I'm impressed, but that'll be tough. I've met a few unfortunate characters there—victims and villains."

"Maybe, but I do speak fluent Spanish."

His eyes widened. "So do I. We could be quite an undercover team, but then we already are."

"Right, Officer Oliver. You and I are servants of the people—as long as we don't get killed in the process."

fifteen

"You're burned," Allison claimed, pressing a finger into Beau's shoulder and noting the white print. "You should have used sunscreen."

Beau lifted his sunglasses to look up at her. "Are you kidding? A tough guy like me? I don't need that stuff."

"Would you like a lecture about the dangers of too much sun?" She glanced down at his chest, the way the muscles molded around his ribs and narrowed into his waist.

"No, thank you, Ma'am. I may be a little pink today, but tomorrow I'll be nice and brown." He replaced his glasses. "By the way, are you admiring my physique?"

Embarrassed, she searched frantically for a rebuttal.

"Thought so." He chuckled. "I may be full of holes, but I can still turn a lady's head."

"Beau!"

He propped himself on his elbows. "Are you denying it?"

She wrinkled her nose at him. "Not exactly."

When he finished laughing, he reached for her hand. "Honestly, I'm the lucky one here. I have the most beautiful woman in the whole world right beside me."

Allison glanced around at a few scantily clad females whose suits left little to the imagination. Not that she wanted to be in anything else but a one-piece suit, but she still felt self-conscious.

"I'm serious," he said, as if reading her mind. "You're gorgeous, intelligent, witty—"

"Keep going," she coaxed.

"And you put up with me."

"There's the clincher."

He planted a kiss on her cheek. "How about a walk along the beach?"

Against the sounds of the waves crashing against the shore and the call of the seagulls, Beau lightly squeezed her hand as they sunk their toes into the sand. She loved the feel of it squishing between her toes.

"We can imagine we're on a desert isle," Beau said, "surrounded by coconut palms and thick green foliage. The water's blue instead of brown, and we don't have to step around the oil spots in the sand." He waved toward the horizon. "In the distance white sails flap in the ocean breeze, and we can taste the salty air."

"Do I detect a bit of a poet in you?" she asked, curiosity gaining the best of her.

"Possibly. I'm a fan of Emerson. 'By the rude bridge that arched the flood / Their flag to April's breeze unfurled / Here once the embattled farmers stood / And fired the shot heard round the world.' "

"You constantly amaze me."

He laughed low. "Someday I'll give you a complete recital."

A twist of a breeze danced off their faces, so refreshing in the sultry sun. She felt absolutely relaxed: no cares or fears. On they walked while she dreamed of the Caribbean.

"You never said. What do you think of my island paradise?" he asked, breaking the silence.

She laughed. "Wonderful. And where is this place?"

He stopped and gazed in the direction of a shrimp boat. "I suppose off the coast of Florida."

"Good. I spent six years in Puerto Rico, and the beaches are exactly as you described. That's where I learned to speak Spanish."

"I learned the hard way, in school."

He released her hand to pick up a seashell, perfectly

shaped without a flaw. *"Usted recoge conchas?"* Do you collect shells? he asked in Spanish.

She studied it as he brushed the sand away. *"Solamente los inusuales."* Only the unusual ones.

"What makes them unusual?" he asked in English.

"When they remind me of people."

He picked up a broken shell and tossed it back into the sand. "Explain your theory."

She bent and picked up the same one he'd just discarded. Holding it in her palm, she began, "I like the irregular-shaped kind, the ones that are rough with ridges and holes, the type you have to wash away the dirt and sand to really see what they look like."

He nodded and grinned. "I see, like people who don't look the part? Like policemen who wear ponytails and earrings?"

"Exactly. It's their heart that makes the difference."

He wrapped his hand around her waist. "Yours definitely has captured mine," he said softly.

Allison felt a delicious tingle race up her spine as he planted a kiss on her neck. Admittedly, she had fallen for this wonderful, unusual, rough-around-the-edges man.

"Hey, what do you say we head home after our walk?" he asked a moment later. "I think I'm burned."

❧

Allison stretched and yawned. The clock on the wall of the Budget Builder read eleven o'clock. One more hour before she could call it a day—or rather a night. In order to take the Fourth of July off this coming week, she agreed to work not only her own day shift from seven to three, but also the afternoon hours from four to twelve tonight.

She stifled another yawn. The extra shift was worth any number of hours. Of course, she might be a bit crabby in the morning, but she'd be spending the entire holiday with Beau and her family.

The Fourth had traditionally been a freedom celebration at her parents' home. Her mom decorated the inside and outside of the house in red, white, and blue banners, streamers, and balloons. She even purchased a trio of petunias to match and planted them by the front door beneath the US flag. She and Dad served foot-long hotdogs, baked beans, potato salad, chips, and whatever else suited their fancy. Homemade ice cream complete with strawberry, chocolate, and blueberry topping hit the dessert line. At the end of the day, they all piled into their cars and headed for a fireworks display.

The last hour dragged by, but finally Allison clocked out and walked from the building with a few other women.

"You ladies want an escort?" the security guard asked.

"No, thanks," one of the women replied. "I think we're all parked close together."

"Okay, but I'm here if you need me," he called.

As they ventured across the parking lot, Allison spotted an unfamiliar truck parked beside her car. "Do any of you own that truck?" she asked.

When no one responded, she stopped and studied it. Enough weird things had happened to her lately to risk making a foolish mistake.

"Let's go ask the manager who owns it," Allison said, straining to read the license plate.

"Why not just get the security guard? I think you're over-reacting," the first woman said.

Allison shrugged. "Maybe so, but unless any of you have been shot lately, then you probably don't understand my precautions." She turned and retraced her steps while the others followed.

"What's the problem?" the guard asked as the women approached him.

"Strange truck parked over there," Allison replied. "Has

the manager left yet?"

"He's still inside. You mean the one driving away?" The guard pointed to a truck leaving the parking lot.

Allison nodded and watched the vehicle speed onto the road and race out of sight. It sounded like a diesel. Maybe she'd acted hastily and paranoid. . .then maybe not.

❧

July Fourth dawned with a downpour predicted for the entire day. Gray clouds rolled across the sky echoing a low rumble and dumping buckets of water on the dry earth as Beau and Allison pulled his truck next to the curb in front of her parents' home. Earlier in the week, Beau accepted their invitation to join them and their brood for a hotdog extravaganza and homemade ice cream. If the rain stopped, they all planned to attend a fireworks display near an elementary school.

Beau viewed Allison's four siblings with a twinge of curiosity—two brothers and two sisters, but he hadn't met any of them before today. She often talked about her family, especially the years her father served in the navy.

With the grandchildren unable to play outside, Allison's mother had set up games and toys on the enclosed porch to keep the children entertained. Their parents mingled with each other and kept an eye on the boisterous group of seven, who longed to be in the sunshine.

Beau found himself assisting a pair of lively, eight-year-old twins, Chad and Christopher, build a space station out of interconnecting, plastic pieces. He thought the project looked easy, especially when he recalled how he used to play with a similar set, but the boys were pros.

"Mr. Beau, try this piece," Chad suggested while Beau struggled through the many shapes and sizes of the building set.

He noted the boy's crystal blue eyes and took the piece, which fit exactly.

The boys' father, Allison's brother-in-law, Tad, joined them on the floor. "Susan and I are grateful for what you did for Allison," he said.

"What did you do, Mr. Beau?" Chad asked, rubbing his freckled nose.

Beau ruffled the boy's hair. "Oh, I helped your aunt Allison when she hurt her arm."

"Oh, yeah, we know about her accident," the boy continued, snapping a wheel into place. "She fell at work and had to go to the hospital for a couple of days."

"She was 'posed to baby-sit us that night but didn't," Christopher said, the mirror of his brother.

Beau glanced up at Tad, who had passed on many of his physical characteristics to his sons. "Allison is a great lady, and you're welcome. Looks like you have a couple of fine sons."

"We think so," Tad replied with a smile. He turned to his sons. "Boys, I'm going to borrow Mr. Beau for a few minutes. We're going to get something to drink."

As Beau struggled to his feet, nearly losing his balance, Tad offered to give him a hand, but he refused. Pride had a lot to do with his independence, although Beau hated to admit it. Once in the kitchen, they poured huge glasses of iced tea.

Tad added sugar to his drink. "Every time I think about the shooting, it makes me angry all over again," he said quietly. "I wonder what happened to the security guard or where Houston's finest were when you and Allison needed them."

"Who knows," Beau replied after a huge gulp of the cold drink. "I'm just glad God allowed me to be there when she needed the help."

Tad pointed to Beau's leg. "How are you doing?"

He chuckled. "All right by the therapist's standards, but mighty slow according to mine."

"How long you off from work?"

"Until the doctor releases me. Probably September."

"What line of work are you in?"

This guy asks as many questions as I do. "Oh, I work for the city."

Tad chuckled and added another spoonful of sugar to his tea. "So, my tax money is supporting you for the rest of the summer?"

Beau grinned. Ordinarily a comment like Tad's would make him bristle, but Allison had said her brother-in-law was blunt. "I'd rather call the cash disability."

He felt an arm slip around his waist and give him a gentle squeeze. The light floral fragrance of his Allison greeted him.

"Is my brother-in-law giving you a bad time?" She snuggled against Beau's shoulder.

"Of course," Tad replied. "I was about to ask him where he went to church, where he worked, his portfolio, and if he made a six-figure income."

Allison's laughter rippled through Beau's spirit. "Good thing I rescued him. Brian and Justin are as bad as you."

Amused, Beau listened to the two banter back and forth. Her brothers hadn't asked many questions at all, neither had her sisters, Susan and Dixie.

"Are you surviving this?" she whispered in his ear once the twins called for their dad. Her warm breath sent crazy messages to his brain.

"You bet. Reminds me of being a kid at family gatherings. I envied my hoards of fun-loving cousins, and they were jealous of me because I didn't have to share my stuff."

"I've always had my brothers and sisters," she said. "Of course, as I said before, I was spoiled rotten, and they didn't want to play with me."

"Spoiled or not, you're my angel," he said, wishing they were alone so he could kiss her.

She grinned. "Thanks for coming today. If this rain doesn't

stop, we can leave whenever you want. I don't want the kids—or Tad—to drive you nuts."

He shook his head. "I'm seeing this party through to the end, even if I get stuck cleaning up."

She sighed deeply and tilted her head, her caramel-colored hair draping like layers of silk on her shoulders. "Tell me, what will things be like when you go back to work?" Everyone else appeared busy and couldn't overhear their quiet conversation.

"I work nights," he said simply, "and I'm off in the middle of the week. The action happens late and on the weekends."

"I'm used to seeing you almost every day. Your odd hours will be an adjustment."

He caught her gaze and the sad reflection in her green eyes. "Can you handle my schedule? Not knowing where I am or what I'm doing?"

She lifted her chin. "Yes. I'm not a quitter. I can make the changes. Besides, I'll be starting school a few weeks before you head back to work."

He welcomed the opportunity to change the topic of conversation. Today he didn't want to discuss the business in the weeks to come, although he needed to face it. "What's involved in your last semester?"

"Hard work," she replied. "The only thing I have left to do is a clinical rotation where I take on a full patient assignment with a staff nurse as my mentor."

"And you'll graduate in December?" he asked, mentally calculating how long they'd be forced to endure each other's hectic pace.

"Uh huh." She laughed. "My first job will most likely be at a hospital, working nights."

He wrapped his arms around her waist. "This will all work out. I promise."

She nodded, but said nothing. More than ever, Beau

wanted to find out who had harassed her. Allison had enough going on in her life without some guy making threatening phone calls.

❧

The following Saturday morning, Allison invited Beau to attend Chad and Christopher's soccer game. Under a sweltering blanket of humidity, the twins' team lost, but a pizza buffet soothed their temporary disappointment. Amidst the video games and seeing friends from school, the little boys' spirits rose to a deafening roar. Allison questioned her sanity in having Beau tag along with the gruesome twosome, as she referred to Chad and Christopher.

"They're heading this way," she whispered to Beau.

"Who? The twins?" He laughed. "I've handled some pretty shady characters. These two are nothing."

"We'll see." She glanced behind them at the advancing troop of eight year olds. "They've brought reinforcements."

"What could they possibly want but a grown-up to play with them?" he asked, downing his soda.

"Mr. Oliver, would you play some video games with us?" Chad asked.

Beau winked at Allison. "See, harmless little boys who are looking for a role model." He turned his attention to the pint-sized soccer team. "Sure, guys, I'll even buy the first couple of games."

Allison shook her head. He'd be singing another tune before the boys were finished with him. The twins, alone, were a handful, and they had half of their team tugging on Mr. Beau.

An hour later, he plopped onto a chair beside her. "I should have listened to you. They wore me out."

She giggled. "Told you. Chad and Christopher are impossible to keep up with, without adding the energy level of a half dozen more."

He raised a brow. "I think I could use them on my next stakeout."

"With or without pepperoni?"

"Without so much energy."

Afterwards, Beau and Allison stopped by his house for a newspaper to see what movies were playing at the theater. Just when they'd decided on a comedy, the doorbell rang.

"It's Kieron," Beau said, as he unlocked the front door.

She instantly recalled his rude mannerisms at the Budget Builder. Call it stubbornness, but Allison couldn't accept Kieron's side of the marriage breakup story. She had nothing to base her opinion on but a feeling, and how could she expect Beau to understand a woman's intuition?

For Beau's sake, she'd be pleasant and try to find something likeable about his neighbor.

"Come in," Beau said, opening wide the door. "Allison and I are heading out to a movie in a few minutes, but we always have time for you."

Kieron flashed his violet gaze at her. She saw a look no decent man should give a woman, and she wanted to sail her hand across his face.

Am I overreacting? Selfish of Beau's time? Jealous of his friends? Lord, help me here. I know I had a bad first impression of Beau's undercover buddies, but not when he explained them to me.

"Hi, Allison. This guy being good to you?" Kieron asked, stepping a bit too close for comfort.

"The best," she replied and hooked arms with Beau.

"I'll only be a minute," Kieron went on, giving Beau his attention. "My TV blew last night, and I wondered if you would tape this afternoon's baseball game. I'm heading out now to get a new TV, but I also need to check some things at the construction site."

Beau waved a hand in protest. "Why don't you watch the

game here? No one will be around anyway. Just lock up and set the alarm when you leave."

Kieron glanced away, then back to Beau. "Are you sure?"

"After all those days you picked up my mail and kept an eye on the place? My home is yours. Help yourself to a soda in the fridge or whatever else you can find."

Kieron pressed his lips together as though he found Beau's offer incredible. "Great. Let me run over to the house and lock up. The game starts in thirty minutes."

Allison watched Kieron dash across the street. Dare she tell Beau about the licentious look he tossed her way? Beau's naïve attitude about his friend irked her. She took a deep breath and walked back into the kitchen. No point in Beau seeing her obvious disgust with his best friend. Besides, her attitude didn't sound very Christian, and she wasn't proud of her thoughts—even if she believed they were true.

"You don't like him at all," Beau stated behind her.

Allison whirled around. He'd jammed his hands into his jeans pocket, his usual sign of frustration. She bit back all the curt remarks she wanted to say about Kieron and swallowed them along with her anger. "Be careful, Beau," she said as gently as possible. "Something about him is not right."

sixteen

Allison left Wednesday night choir rehearsal exhilarated with the music they'd practiced for Sunday and the realization she and Beau were sharing a fabulous summer. Each time they met confirmed their relationship, and even their few squabbles resulted in a stronger bond. The one issue they failed to agree upon was Kieron Bates.

She didn't like him. She didn't trust him. Something about the man was evil, but Beau refused to consider that his old friend might have made improper advances to Allison or lied about his wife. To Allison, if a man lied about one thing, he'd lie about another.

Pulling her car onto the main street, she drove toward home, but a sudden urge for a cold drink and fries caused her to swing into a fast food restaurant and head for the drive-thru. A late model truck eased in behind her—no doubt, the munchies had hit that driver too.

After giving her order, she moved ahead to the cashier window, handed the young man her money, and grabbed her fries and drink. Odd, the truck behind her didn't pick up any food. She glanced in her rearview mirror but couldn't see the driver because he wore a cowboy hat.

She shrugged and headed home. The truck followed her. A moment later, he turned the same way she did. He must live in her neighborhood. Still, she didn't like the way he rode her bumper. Feeling a bit apprehensive, she signaled a right turn and drove down a street away from her general direction. He followed.

Suddenly she remembered the truck parked at the Budget

135

Builder when she pulled a late shift. Could it be the same?

Allison's pulse rose, and her mouth felt dry. She jammed the straw into her soda and took a drink. All the while, she noted the truck trailing behind her.

She signaled left, and he turned with her. Allison's body trembled. The shooting and the phone threats rose like an erupting volcano in front of her eyes. Clumsily, she locked her doors and yanked the cell phone from her purse. Using speed dial, she punched in Beau's home number.

It rang once, twice. *Please, Beau, pick up.* Three times. The answering machine started to play his message. She swallowed hard, biting back the tears and yet feeling the panic seize her quivering body. At least he had caller ID and would recognize her number.

Oh, Lord, help me. I don't know what to do!

Allison stepped on the gas and sped through the residential area, but the truck stayed right behind her. Once she tried to capture a look of his face, but the cowboy hat hid any visible features. Frightened and uncertain of what to do, she searched the area for a police car. At least if an officer stopped her for speeding, she'd be safe.

If only she'd taken the time to program Beau's new cell number into her phone. In the darkness, accompanied with her rather reckless driving, she couldn't pull the number from her purse or dial it in the dark. For certain she needed to get out of the neighborhood before she hit something or someone.

At the next stop sign, she turned onto a major thoroughfare while the truck rode her bumper. Pressing ahead to the next corner, she turned right onto a four-lane street. Surely she could lose him now. Her phone rang, rattling her senses, and she hastily picked it up.

"Hi, Baby, sorry I missed your call; I was outside with Kieron."

She burst into tears, barely able to speak. "A truck is

following me," she finally managed through chattering teeth.

"Are you sure?" he asked, his tone filled with concern.

"Oh, yes. Since I left the church, he's been on my bumper. I've even wound through a subdivision, but he's still behind me. Now, I'm on Louetta, just before 249, and I don't even see a police car to help me. There aren't any at the gas stations, the convenience stores, nothing."

"Listen, head my way. I'll be standing outside." His voice sounded calm against the roaring of her frenzied mind.

"Okay. I'm not that far." She swerved into the next lane to miss a car. Perspiration trickled down the side of her face, but she couldn't swipe it with the phone in one hand and the steering wheel in the other. Praise God, she no longer wore the sling, yet the arm grasping the steering wheel ached.

"Don't hang up the phone. Lay it on the seat if you need to, but keep me on the line. How close are you now?"

She took a deep breath and blinked her eyes to clear her vision. "About ten minutes or so at the speed I'm going."

"Can you see his face?"

She snatched another glimpse. "No, he's wearing a hat and driving a big pickup. And he's too close for me to read his license plates."

"Don't worry about that, Allison. Just continue to drive my way," he stated calmly.

"Please, keep talking to me. I'm afraid I'll lose it if you don't." She shivered while her hands felt clammy.

"You can do this," he went on. His gentleness was a blessing as she battled her hysteria.

"It has a diesel engine," she managed through chattering teeth.

"Good girl. That will help us later in filing a police report. Ignore him and simply concentrate on the road."

A thought plunged into her mind. "Do you. . .do you think he's the man who threatened me? Or someone from the shooting?" She sucked in her breath. Control. She had to find control.

"Honey, he's probably some kid who saw a good-looking girl and is all caught up in the chase. He's banking on you being scared and wrecking your little blue car."

His evaluation didn't soothe her nerves or stop the truck behind her. "I don't believe your lame explanation for one minute. I know this whole thing is connected—the shooting, the phone threats—and I know you're hiding things from me." Her rise of tone startled her. "I'm sorry. This is not your fault."

"Honey, I don't have any more information than when I left the hospital," he replied. "But I promise I'll get to the bottom of this—"

"If we live through it."

"Allison, don't even think such a thing. God is looking out for us."

She bit back a sob. "I'm sorry, and I know God's protecting both of us."

"Now I hear your spunk. Where are you?"

"Turning into your subdivision." She heard him sigh. "He's right behind me." She sped on, but when she took a left at Beau's street, the truck raced past her. "He's gone," she whispered.

"The rat knew where you were headed," Beau muttered.

Once in his driveway, she flung aside the seatbelt and jumped from her car into the comfort of his arms. All the while she cried, repeatedly telling herself to calm down. God had protected her. The ordeal was over, at least for the moment.

As her tears subsided, she relaxed until she could pull herself from Beau's embrace. Fright and anger coursed through her veins at the man who bullied her. She desperately wanted answers and the assurance that those who had made her life and Beau's a living nightmare had been apprehended. Then she wrapped her arms around him and felt it—a gun tucked into his belt at the small of his back.

Allison shuddered. As though Beau read her thoughts, he drew her back into his arms.

"I'm a cop," he said, reaching for her hand hanging limply at her side. "He could have stopped in front of the house and opened fire."

This part of his life sounded so foreign to her. She'd never seen him in a police uniform or with a gun, and he didn't even wear a bullet-proof vest when on the streets. He'd told her about his job, the endless waiting, the getting to know people, and how he and Ace often worked together until they built up enough trust to buy narcotics.

Beau, as an undercover cop, had a lifestyle far from her realm of understanding. Reality hit her hard. She recoiled at his touch, the memory of the shooting, and the crimson pools of blood vivid in her mind.

He's a trained officer. He knows how to use a gun. This is what he does while the rest of the world sleeps, and soon he'll return to it.

"Are you all right?" he asked against the sound of singing crickets and the canopy of a star-studded sky.

"I. . .I think so. I just want to wake up and find out this horrible nightmare is over." She wanted to find reassurance on his face, but she couldn't forget the touch of cold metal against her fingertips.

Lord, help me overcome this fear. I don't want to shut Beau out because of my inability to handle his using a gun.

Slowly her gaze moved upward to his face. The faint glow from the streetlight outlined his rugged features, and she slowly brought her hand to his cheek. "You are the last one I want to take out my frustrations on," she whispered.

"I understand," he said and kissed the hand caressing him. "Let's go inside. I'll put the gun away and call Sarge."

She nibbled at her lip. "I never told you this, but the night I worked until midnight, a strange truck was parked next to my car when I left. When I walked back to talk to the manager and security guard about it, the truck left. I think it might have been the same one. Beau, I want us to pray about tonight. . .and everything else."

He retrieved the gun from the small of his back before taking a long look up and down the street. He slipped one arm around her waist and gave her a gentle squeeze. Gently, he shepherded her to the back door, to light, and safety.

Inside the house, he set his gun on top of the refrigerator and grasped her hands with his. "We need to pray before we do another thing." When she agreed, he began, "Lord, we aren't sure what happened here tonight, if it's connected to my old case or the shooting. But we know You do, and we're giving all our fears and questions to You in faith and trust. We are clinging to the cross and Your promise to never forsake us in times of want and need. Give us wisdom and strength to meet each day with the supernatural joy that comes only from You. In Jesus' precious and holy name, amen."

She stepped into his arms and basked in the strength of the godly man sheltering her. She felt God's presence whispering His peace and offering hope for a victory won on the cross. "Thank you," she whispered. "Lately I forget God has a purpose in all of this. I needed the reminder."

He weaved his fingers through her hair, resting his head atop hers. "Sometimes I think I shouldn't see you anymore— that my involvement with you invited those threats. Except, now I believe we've been thrown into some sort of crucible, and we're bound by another force to stick it out."

She feigned a smile. "I wish I had your bravery."

He kissed the top of her head. "I'm not so brave."

She felt the rise and fall of his even breathing and heard his heart pounding in her ears.

"When those guys are in jail and you have absolutely

nothing to fear, I want to talk to you about another matter. Right now, I have a case to solve," he said.

"We," she reminded him, "we're in this together."

"Of course. Just remember the bodyguard in me wants to protect you from all of this, and I'm not doing a very good job."

"And the independent side of me says I don't need you risking your life for my sake."

He hugged her close. "What we both need is to rely on the one and only protector. The invincible." He brushed his finger across her lips. "As much as I like holding you, I'd better call Sarge and see if he has a clue about the road hog."

She glanced at the phone and saw the answering machine flashed a message. He reached across the kitchen counter and depressed the play button.

"Pretty little Allison okay?" The man laughed low. "I just needed to make sure you were keeping your end of the bargain. Beau, if you value Allison's lovely little neck, don't double-cross me."

seventeen

"Will it ever end?" Allison uttered. "What more could they want?"

Anger surged through Beau's body as he quickly checked his caller-ID. Naturally the caller had the number blocked. He clenched his fists and gritted his teeth. He wanted to curse like the street people he normally kept company with, to run his fist through a window—all the things contrary to his faith. He wanted nothing more than to get his hands on the source of her fear and tear him apart. Nothing had changed. He'd gone through the motions of abandoning the case, but it hadn't stopped the culprits from frightening an innocent young woman.

Who were these guys? If he'd been so close to uncovering them, he should have a lead. Instead, he looked like an idiot, while the woman he loved stood before him, trembling. He'd cracked harder cases than this—one involving a member of city council and another where a woman laundered her money through a mission.

Oh, Lord, You gave me a mind and a heart for police work. Am I not listening? What am I doing wrong?

"I hate what this is doing to you," he finally said, viewing the tension through the stiffened muscles in her body. "I promise you, I will find out who is responsible for this."

She shook her head and swallowed. "If I'm terrified, imagine how others feel who don't have the Lord. Beau, I want you to do whatever is necessary to stop these horrible men."

Her declaration irritated him. "Don't you think I am? I'm on this case night and day."

"But what about your old contacts? Have your friends been able to get information from them?" She crossed her arms as though she could hide the viciousness plaguing her.

"You've been watching too many police shows," he said, releasing her to pick up his new cell phone and call Sarge.

"I'm simply thinking about what you've already told me about your job. You said it took a long time to win people's trust. Those cops assigned to your case haven't had time to develop friendships, and you and I know the drug guys are far too clever to risk getting caught."

He frowned, his anger threatening to go out of control. "What do you want me to do? If I'm officially on the case, don't you understand I may as well invite them to put a bullet in your head?"

"No! I'm simply saying what you're doing is not enough. Protecting me has become an obsession rather than doing your job." She glared at him as though waiting for his reaction before she exploded.

He threw the phone down and grabbed her shoulders. "Don't you know I love you? I can't let anything happen to you."

Her eyes widened, and she paled. He'd frightened her with his fury. Instantly, he released her arms. "Alli, I'm sorry. I had no right to grab you."

She rubbed her flesh where he'd squeezed much too hard. "What did you say?" she asked slowly.

"I said I'm sorry." He sighed heavily. "I care about you; I love you. Nothing matters to me except your safety."

A tear trickled from her eye. "And I love you." She wiped away the wetness. "I'm no help to you at all. In fact, I'm in the way of everything you're trying to do. If not for me, those guys would be in jail." She hesitated, her sea green pools filled with emotion. "And because I love you, I can't stand idly by, helpless and scared like some rabbit. Beau, you have a job to do, and it's not being my bodyguard."

"Honey, these guys play for keeps. I can't do any more than what I'm doing now. So help me, I'll find out who they are and get them put where they belong."

Hours later, after Allison had received a police escort home, Beau paced the living room. Alone in the dark, he playcd and replayed every word, every scene surrounding the drug case. Whatever the answer, it had to be something so obvious that he ignored it. He felt so stupid, so insignificant, totally broken.

First thing in the morning, he'd call Sarge and request another criminal history check on Joe Lopez. This time he wouldn't let anything slip by him. He knew a link existed, something he had repeatedly missed.

He glanced across the street at Kieron's dark house. Snippets of their times together in high school flashed across his mind. Kieron had gotten into a little more trouble than Beau, but nothing serious. Then he remembered the car theft. Odd he'd forgotten, but it happened after Beau had come to know the Lord. Kieron wasn't interested in Jesus, and they'd started to go their separate ways. Kieron's dad had gotten him out of the trouble, but later Beau saw his old friend still kept bad company. After graduation, he'd lost track.

Beau shook his head. Those old recollections of Kieron bothered him—his friend, his neighbor, the guy who watched his house and got his mail while he recuperated in the hospital, the same man who cried buckets when his wife left him for another man. His bud.

The one person who knew his job as an undercover cop.

A twist of uneasiness settled upon him like the deadly calm before a twister. Allison didn't care for Kieron, although she tried to mask her real feelings for Beau's sake. He saw the words unsaid and her obvious dislike and distrust. Plus she believed Lori's story. Maybe he ought to talk to Lori again and make sure her reasons for leaving matched Kieron's.

Oh, Lord, what if I've been wrong? I hate the thought of making excuses for a man who lives on the wrong side of the law. Forgive me, Lord. Give me wisdom to end this thing.

Nine o'clock the next morning, Beau searched through the junk drawer in his kitchen for Lori's parents' number. She'd given it to him at the grocery, and he'd stuck it on the side of the refrigerator, but somehow her number had disappeared.

Lori, Kieron, and Beau had all gone to high school together, but Beau could not remember her maiden name. Finally he gave up and dragged down his school annual from the attic. Just when he thought his leg had healed nicely, he attempted something to prove otherwise. Climbing up and down the attic ladder highlighted one of those moments.

He dialed the Hayley number with a mixture of curiosity and regret. The last thing he wanted to find out was his old friend had lied.

An hour later, he pulled up in front of Lori's parents' home. The huge New Orleans–style home brought back a flood of memories from high school days. Her parents had opened their doors to every teenager who needed a listening ear, a meal, or someplace to stay for a night. Mr. and Mrs. Hayley had one standing rule: If you stayed over on Saturday, you attended church on Sunday. No excuse. Beau had almost forgotten their hospitality and Christian beliefs.

He chuckled and opened his car door. It would be nice to see Lori's parents again. Too bad the visit couldn't be under more pleasant circumstances.

Lori greeted him at the door. She looked even bigger than before, like a balloon ready to pop. "Mom and Dad just left for an appointment," she said. "They wanted to see you, but perhaps another time. Come on in."

"Tell them I said hello," Beau said, feeling a bit awkward. "When's the baby due?"

"Two weeks," she said with a smile. She patted her

rounded stomach. "She's kicking me to pieces today. Most likely wanting to get out of there."

Beau laughed. "I suppose you have a name picked out."

With her hand resting on her stomach, she said, "Sure do. Bethany Lynn."

"That's a pretty name. Let me know when she gets here." He detected the tantalizing aroma of cookies. "Does your mother still bake like she used to?"

"Always," Lori replied, smiling. "It doesn't help my waistline. Grab some cookies on your way through the kitchen." She gestured toward the family room. The old, denim sofa had been replaced with a cream-colored leather one, and the chipped and scratched tables were now chrome and glass. Even the food stains on the carpet had vanished. "Sit down and tell me what brings you here today."

He sunk down on the sofa. "To talk about Kieron."

Lori frowned. "I hope you're not here to persuade me to move back with him."

"Not at all." Suddenly he felt uncomfortable with the questions probing his mind.

"Would you like something to drink?"

"Don't think so, but thanks." The cookies had lost their appeal with what he needed to find out. He watched her move awkwardly toward an easy chair and wondered if she needed help.

"Glad I don't have much more of this waiting left," she said. "Beau, why are you so nervous?"

He leaned forward and folded his hands. "I've some serious questions about Kieron."

"Is he all right?" Her forehead wrinkled.

"Sure, as far as I know." *You're not being truthful.*

She placed a hand on her bulging stomach, like she'd done at the grocery store as though protecting her baby from what she needed to say. Taking a deep breath, she began,

"Remember all the fun we had in school? College days were great, but not like being young with all our friends."

Beau smiled. "Great times. I think in college we all had different agendas; I did, anyway. I always thought I could go back to those old high school days, but they're gone forever."

Lori closed her eyes. "Kieron always had such wild ideas, and he was incredibly funny. I used to love his impersonations. He could do anyone, facial contortions and all."

"Yeah. He had us all in stitches most of the time," Beau replied, then nodded. "He had all the teachers pegged."

An uncomfortable silence followed.

"Have you seen him high?" Lori finally asked.

He shook his head. "Never an indication, which bothers me. What you told me at the grocery sounded. . .rather bizarre."

"Kieron hid his habit from me for a long time, but I found out for sure after getting pregnant—or I wouldn't have risked a baby's health. I have no idea how long he's been a user— probably about three years."

"Three years?"

"That's when I first started noticing the mood swings and money disappearing. I thought his roofing business was doing badly, but when I checked into the records, I found out the opposite."

"Did you ask him about the missing money?"

"Yes, and he exploded. Then we started having more cash again, and I felt better for a long time. I ignored the mood swings and thought he felt trapped in our marriage. He mentioned starting a family, so I assumed a baby would take care of the problems."

"So then you caught him high?" Beau asked.

"Several times." Her gaze flitted about the room. "Something else too. One day, as a surprise, I cleaned out his office. You can't imagine how messy a contractor's office can be.

Anyway I found a huge amount of money in the back of a drawer."

"How much?"

"One hundred thousand dollars," she whispered, as though someone in the house might hear. "Took me a long time to ask him about it. Frankly, I was scared."

A strange feeling curled in the pit of his stomach. "What did he say?"

"He very calmly said he'd been saving the money for a new home for us and the baby. I wanted to know why he hadn't deposited it into a bank, and he said he didn't trust them." Lori swallowed hard. "I didn't believe him and told him so. I demanded to know where the cash came from, but he lost his temper and told me never to go through his private things again. He stormed out. Several hours later he returned home, apologized, and left again. When he came back this time, he was high."

"Did you two talk then?"

"No. I waited until a few days later. I gave him an ultimatum—the drugs or me and the baby. You know the rest."

Beau took a deep breath. "Do you have any idea where the cash came from?"

She hesitated, and a tear rolled down her cheek. "I have my suspicions, Beau, but they're too awful to even say."

He nodded, understanding completely. He didn't want to believe it either. "Have any shady-looking characters ever been to see him?"

She nibbled at her lip, and he waited for her to respond. "No, but some of his employees look like he scraped the bottom of the barrel to find them," she replied. "Beau, I need to know why he said I left."

"Does it matter?"

"I still love him. He has a substance abuse problem, and because of that I won't subject our baby to his mood swings or his illegal habit." She stared at her hands, then lifted her head. "What he's told people is important to me."

Beau hesitated a moment longer. "He said you left him for another man."

Lori didn't flinch. "I'm not surprised. He accused me of an affair whenever we quarreled. He even suggested the baby belonged to you." Her gaze bore into his. "I've never been unfaithful. Kieron has been my life."

The look in her eyes told him she'd spoken the truth. "I understand, Lori. I'm sorry to have upset you, but I needed to know the truth."

Her eyes pooled with tears. "It's the law, isn't it? Kieron is in terrible trouble. I just feel it."

eighteen

Allison nervously flipped on her turn signal and whipped her car into the left lane. The beat-up vehicle behind her followed. Her stomach churned with the memory of the last time a truck trailed her. The car stayed on her bumper as it had for the past several minutes, ever since she finished her shift at the Budget Builder. Up ahead she needed to turn left and swerved into that lane. A yellow light quickly flashed red, bringing her to a halt. Beau had therapy this afternoon, or she'd head in his direction. She glanced into her rearview mirror and saw the other car had swung in behind her. She also grabbed a glimpse of the driver and passengers: a carload of teens laughing and pointing at her.

Relieved, she relaxed slightly and focused her attention on the traffic light. Kids. They must have just gotten out of school and were in a hurry. For a few moments, she thought she'd been followed again. When had she become so paranoid? And this wasn't the first time she'd panicked in traffic. Lately, every vehicle seemed to represent danger. She wanted this nightmare ended now.

At times she feared her attraction to Beau centered around the danger they faced together. He'd mentioned that facet of their relationship before, but when she thought of not having him in her life, a deep sense of loss pierced her heart. And it had nothing to do with police work. Her feelings had everything to do with love, the kind God intended for a man and a woman.

Her thoughts drifted back to the night Beau told her he loved her.

"When this is all over," he'd said, "I'd like for you and me to sit down and talk."

"You've said this before. What are we going to discuss?" she'd asked.

"The future—and what it might hold for us." The earnest look on his face had told her he wanted God's best.

"We can discuss it anytime," she had replied.

He had shaken his head and drawn her into his arms. "No. I don't want you making a decision until those guys are in jail. Right now I'd be afraid you were thinking in terms of the danger we've shared rather than what God intends for us. In the meantime, don't forget I love you."

Allison touched her lips, remembering the kiss sealing his words. They'd known each other for a little more than four months, but she couldn't imagine her life without him. She let her thoughts dance with the years ahead, Beau continuing in his police work and she fulfilling her own ministry as a nurse.

The love swelling in her heart brought an errant tear. She snatched up her cell phone and punched in the code to his house.

"Hi, it's Allison. I'm checking in to see how you're doing. Hope today's session went well. I'll be home until seven o'clock. This is choir night. I'll give you a call around nine-fifteen from my cell—depends on how long I talk afterwards. Oh, Mom called and invited us to dinner Friday night. Check your schedule and let me know. Bye, love you."

The mention of her mother left a path of regret. She and Allison had always been extremely close, but since the shooting, their conversations wavered between deceit and superficial. She couldn't tell her about the threats, at least not until arrests were made.

&

Beau examined the criminal history check and the additional

data put together about Joe Lopez. By using the man's social security number, the police department could secure a wealth of information. Although Beau had read most of the background material before, he needed to refresh his memory.

Born and raised on the southeast side of town. In and out of trouble since the age of fifteen. Arrested twice for possession. Done time for theft. Sister lives in San Antonio. Parents deceased. He'd worked construction with a string of companies, one of them, Bates Roofing, until about eighteen months ago.

Bingo.

Finally he saw a connection between the shooting and the narcotics case. Kieron's involvement with Lopez infuriated him. No doubt with Beau's house key, he had access to everything: Beau's phone numbers, laptop files, his undercover buds stopping by, the ability to watch him come and go. Everything Kieron needed to continue dodging the system lay right there at his fingertips. Beau felt like a rookie cop, more so a fool. But why had Lopez come after Allison? That part still didn't make sense. But Lopez had been high—confused and disoriented.

Unless Joe Lopez had been after Beau and not Allison.

Snatching up his cell phone, Beau punched in Sarge's number.

"I think I've figured out most of it," he said, and proceeded to tell him about the connection between Joe Lopez and Kieron Bates, including Lori's reasons for leaving her husband.

"Your best friend, huh?" Sarge said. "We knew it had to be someone on the inside."

Guilt washed over Beau. "I'm going over to see him tonight. Try to talk some sense into his thick skull. I have no idea how deep he's in with this—hate to even speculate."

"You're going to need backup," Sarge said.

"Right. But give me lots of time. He doesn't get home until

seven-thirty or after, and I want to ease into this, hopefully get a confession."

He heard Sarge tap his pen against the desk. "All right, we'll keep a surveillance on the house, starting about eight. It's your call, but if we don't hear anything from you by nine-thirty, we're coming in."

Beau hung up and punched in Allison's number. He waited for the answering machine to pick up.

"Alli, it's Beau. Are you there?"

"Hi. Did you have a good day?" The musical lilt of her voice temporarily erased what he needed to do that evening.

"I think so. Listen, Honey, I may have this case wrapped up tonight."

"You're kidding. Oh, Beau, what wonderful news. I can't believe it. What has happened?"

"I'll tell you all about it later, but for right now I could use a few prayers."

"Beau," she said slowly, "this is dangerous, isn't it?"

He heard the panic. "Not for a veteran like me."

Silence met him. "What time are you leaving? I might stay home from choir rehearsal tonight."

"No, please go on to church. Remember, this is my life, what I do every day. In about a month, I'll be back on the streets again."

She paused. "I understand, and I'll be praying while I'm singing."

"It'll be late before I can get back to you," he said.

"I don't care. I won't be able to sleep, anyway."

Beau laid his phone on the kitchen counter. *Lord, this is going to be tough, and I need You with me. I pray for Kieron. He needs You. I pray for a clear head and Your words in my mouth. Protect me from evil and let me represent You. In Jesus' name, amen.*

Shortly before eight o'clock, Beau stood outside Kieron's

door and contemplated the reality of his best friend being knee-deep in drugs. Anger coursed through him as he considered the death of Joe Lopez, the phone calls to Allison, and the countless other people who were dead or addicted to drugs. No matter what Beau's past or present relationship might be with Kieron, the drug ring had to be stopped.

The cop side of him felt decisively stupid for not detecting the warning signals. Allison had been on to Kieron from the beginning, while Beau tossed the obvious aside. He didn't like his suspicions about a few other things either. He didn't want to believe any of it, but if Kieron had money hidden about his office, then he knew way too much about the narcotics game.

Beau rang Kieron's doorbell. He glanced at the untrimmed shrubbery and weed-infested flowerbeds. Last summer Beau and Lori competed with yard work and flowers, which probably led Kieron to accuse her of infidelity. The idea disgusted him. He knew a time when they were like brothers, but brothers didn't do what Kieron suspected of Beau.

"Hey. Come on in," Kieron said, hosting a wide grin. "Want to join me for a couple of burgers?"

"Sure." Beau limped along behind him to the kitchen. The house looked like no one had done anything to it in months—probably since Lori left. Clothes were strewn everywhere along with fast-food bags, drinking glasses, and newspapers. All of the blinds and drapes were drawn, and the smell of spoiled food and filth lingered in the air like a bad omen.

"What have you been up to?" Kieron asked, opening the refrigerator and removing a package of hamburger patties.

Beau feigned a chuckle and eased into a chair at the kitchen table. "Looking after my yard, driving to therapy, and slowly working on building a new patio."

"Such a life. While I'm working in the hot sun, you're in air-conditioned comfort, living an easy life." He smiled easily: Kieron, the charmer.

"Not all the time. I did see Lori today," Beau said casually.

"Oh?" Kieron asked, lifting a brow. "How is she?"

"Very pregnant. Of course she told me you already knew."

Kieron nodded and turned his back. "The brat has to belong to her new boyfriend."

"Lori said the baby is yours. She's living with her parents and claimed she never had a boyfriend."

Kieron shrugged. "He must have booted her out."

"Whatever. She said a few other interesting things too. She said you two had some serious problems that you refused to face." Beau felt calm, amazingly calm, the kind of peace only God orchestrated.

"Like what?" Kieron asked, pulling a bottle of Worcestershire sauce from a cabinet. He twisted off the lid and doused the patties.

"She said you had a drug problem and refused to get help. That's why she moved out."

He whirled around to face Beau, his features strained. "Women. You give them the best you have, and they make up garbage. Leave 'em alone—that's my advice. Even your pretty little Allison will turn on you. Wait and see."

Beau felt his stomach curdle. The way Kieron spit out "pretty little Allison" triggered an alarm. He'd heard the voice before—at the other end of the phone. Kieron's impersonations.

"So you're the one," Beau said as evenly as discussing the weather. "You made the phone calls to Alli."

Kieron forced a laugh. "What phone calls are you talking about? First you come over here with some wild accusations you heard from Lori, and now you accuse me of threatening your girlfriend."

Beau stood, his fists clenched. "I never said the calls were threatening."

A slow smile spread over Kieron's face, and he stepped over to a drawer. "Right you are. Looks like you and I are finished with our little conversation." He whipped out a revolver and pointed it at Beau. "I think you'll be staying awhile."

"You don't want to do this," Beau said, staring straight into Kieron's violet eyes. "It's not too late to turn this thing around. I can help you."

He sneered. "Why would I want to go to jail when I'm making a small fortune?"

"Supplying narcotics to kids and users?" Beau asked. The truth cut him like a knife. He never wanted to believe Kieron was capable of destroying lives.

"You bet. Easy bucks when you're smart. I thought I'd died and gone to heaven when you moved in. What a stupid cop. You played into my every move—giving me a key to your place and letting me know where and when you went on duty."

Beau took a step forward. He needed to shorten the distance between them.

"Don't move." Kieron's tone took on a deadly sound.

"I've got a backup team outside. They're coming in whether you give yourself up or not."

"Liar," Kieron said. He pulled a roll of duct tape from the drawer. "Have a seat. You're not going anywhere."

Beau settled back into the chair; no point in pushing Kieron into pulling the trigger. Backups didn't do a dead man a bit of good.

Kieron whipped Beau's hands behind the chair and wrapped the tape tightly around his wrists, chest, and feet. He pulled Beau's phone from his pocket and tossed it on the table. "Good old duct tape," he said, with a sneer, "has a million uses."

"You're already caught, Kieron. I'm telling you, it's only a matter of time before they move in. You can give yourself up, and things will go easier."

"Not hardly. I suppose you want me to pray about it?" He snorted. "Think about it. Your God doesn't have much clout with me, and all He's done for you is make sure you were filled with lead and made to look like a fool."

"There's more to God than that."

Kieron waved the gun in front of his face. "I've heard enough."

"What about Lori and the baby? You're throwing away your future with a woman who loves you," Beau said, stalling for time. "Think about it. What good is the money without your family?"

A flicker of compassion spread over Kieron's face. He did love his wife. "She made her choice," he said gruffly, as though denying his feelings. "Her loss."

"Lori still loves you."

"She has a strange way of showing it. I'm moving on to bigger things." Kieron's face hardened. "Does Allison know about your coming over here tonight?"

Beau shook his head, disgust filling his senses. "Don't drag her into this."

"She's been involved all along. I can't have her running around with information, now can I?"

"She doesn't know a thing," Beau said, fighting to control his voice. "Leave her alone."

Kieron rubbed his chin. "You're not in any position to tell me what to do, but I do need to have the latest on your case."

"There isn't anything to tell," Beau muttered, wishing he'd asked for the backup sooner.

"Maybe I haven't made myself clear. Either you tell me, or Allison is dead. Then we'll talk about your parents. I have a business to run, standards to maintain."

"So you're the one heading up the whole thing." The realization made Beau feel even more stupid—and angry.

"Right, Buddy. I'm your man."

Beau tugged at the tape binding his hands. "I've been off the case for weeks. You know that."

"I know you, and you don't give up on anything." Kieron set a frying pan on the stove and switched on the gas burner. "I'll give you time to think while I cook up these burgers."

"I hate to disappoint you, but there's nothing to tell."

Long moments passed in silence. Beau's wrists grew numb with the tape cutting deep into his wrists. He struggled, but the binding held him tight against the chair.

The frying meat spit and splattered while the aroma wafted across the kitchen. Time was running out. Beau needed to think of something to appease Kieron.

"You waited too long." Kieron scooped up the burgers and dumped them onto a couple of open buns. He reached inside the fridge and pulled out a bottle of ketchup.

"I already said I'm off the case." Beau gritted his teeth to keep from lashing out. *Oh, Lord, help me.*

Picking up a burger, Kieron licked the thick, red ketchup oozing from the bun. He picked up his cell phone and punched in a number. "Yeah, she's at the church until nine. Set it up, and call me back."

Beau watched Kieron greedily devour both burgers. He tore into the sandwich like a wild animal devouring the flesh of a lesser creature.

Repulsion for his old friend snaked through Beau's body. How could Kieron be so evil and Beau have not recognized the warning signs? At that moment, Beau despised himself. He knew Kieron had arranged something for Allison's demise. *God help her. Stop him before anyone else is killed.*

Kieron's cell rang, and he snatched it up. "Good," he said. "Go on home, and I'll call you later." He set the phone on the counter and tossed Beau a triumphant smile. "A bomb's been planted in Allison's car. I told you I meant business."

nineteen

Allison placed her sheet music into the allotted slot for Sunday morning. She glanced at her watch: eight forty-five. The music minister had let them out early. She'd prayed for Beau all evening, finding it difficult to concentrate on choir rehearsal. The sooner she got home the better, and this was not a night to stay and visit. The drive home took ten minutes, but she wanted to be there now.

The thought of the past four months' nightmare nearly being over filled her with a mixture of joy and panic. Whatever Beau was doing had to be risky, because he'd called and asked specifically for prayer.

This part of Beau's life plagued her. Before the shooting, she hadn't met an undercover policeman. They existed in news reports and thriller movies, but not in her perfectly contented world. It wasn't until the night she saw his gun that she understood the gravity of his work. He lived in danger due to reality; she lived safely because of his commitment. The world could be an ugly place if given over to the degradation of men's minds without the Lord. Beau had been trained to protect and serve the innocent and rid the streets of crime. God forbid if she ever took him or any other police officer for granted.

She knew for certain her love for Beau didn't stem from gratitude. Those misgivings faded into obscurity when she learned his heart. He had a ministry as valid as her pastor, her Sunday school teacher, or the missionary sent to a third world country. She couldn't ever ask him to quit; neither did she want to. She loved Beau—who he was and what he viewed as his life calling. She must learn to trust God for his safety, but in times like these, that aspect was so hard.

She moved through the crowd of choir members toward the exit, greeting them, but hardly making any small talk. Preoccupied with Beau, she found socializing nearly impossible. After all, she couldn't tell any of them about it.

"Are you okay?" Sandy asked, with a tilt of her head.

"Oh, sure. I'm just tired and have a ton of things on my mind." *Now I've lied to my best friend.*

"Do you want to grab a cup of coffee and talk?"

Allison forced a smile. "No, thanks. I think I'll head home and get to bed early."

Walking toward the front door, Allison dug through her purse for her keys. She gripped them tightly and checked her cell phone: no messages. Within ten feet of her car, she stood ready to disarm the security system and suddenly had an urge to go back inside the church to pray for Beau. She paused for a moment, then retraced her steps. She entered the worship center and slipped into a pew. A muted light shone above the choir loft, illuminating a purple banner that read, "He is Lord." Sunday the area would be filled with two hundred voices praising God in song, but right now, she needed the solace of His peace.

For the next few minutes, she read from a Bible inserted on the back of the pew. She leafed through the Psalms and prayed many of them. Tears welled her eyes and a sense of urgency needled at her heart.

Lord, I've repeatedly asked You what You desire of my relationship with Beau. Ever since he's entered my life, I've felt Your hand in all we do. The danger has been devastating, but I've never felt alone. You were there with me then, just as You are here with me now. I pray for Your protection over Beau. Give him a clear mind and courage to do the tasks You have placed before him. Lord, I need courage and stamina to stand beside him. He's a soldier in a war zone, but You are his light.

Suddenly the sound of an explosion startled her. She jumped up, nearly dropping the Bible. At first she thought the noise came from another part of the church, then she realized it had to be outside. Not sure how long she'd prayed, Allison feared for the safety of her friends. She hurried from the worship center into the large atrium where glass doors led to the parking lot.

Allison caught her breath too frightened to scream. Her car had burst into flames. A moment later, another explosion shattered what little remained of it.

৯৹

Beau twisted his wrists in an effort to loosen the tape binding his numbed hands. Although he'd succeeded in gaining more mobility, he still was nowhere near freeing himself. Every moment ticking by increased his anxiety. Every thought became a prayer for Allison's life. Some bodyguard he'd turned out to be. He'd led his precious Alli right to the grave, and he couldn't do anything about it. His gaze wandered about the kitchen for a clock. The microwave read two o'clock, the oven below it read six. The actual time had to be nearly nine.

Lord, I don't care about me. It's Allison I'm begging for. Please, stop them from planting that bomb in her car. If only my backup would step in sooner. Oh, Lord, I'm rambling. I'm scared. I'm trusting in Your mighty power and deliverance.

"Can't you leave Allison out of this?"

"Don't think so," Kieron said. "She got in the way of things when Joe followed you into the Budget Builder."

"So he was after me." Being right didn't stop the ache in his heart for Allison.

Kieron nodded and swallowed hard. "You got it. Remember the last buy you made the night before? They nearly led you to my door. Couldn't have them give away my cover, could I?"

"But why involve her in the first place?"

Kieron shrugged. "I found out Joe took a hit before he entered the store. Seeing her must have confused him."

"You nearly killed an innocent woman." Beau clenched his jaw. "How many others, Kieron?"

"Not sure. I tried to get you once, but Joe blew it," Kieron replied, leaning against the counter. "This time there won't be any mistake."

"Doesn't murder bother you?"

"Naw. I've done it before; I'll do it again."

Beau wrestled with the raging thoughts threatening to push him over the brink of sanity. If given the opportunity, he'd tear Kieron apart piece by piece.

Allison, his precious angel. How could anyone want to hurt her? He loved her innocence, her total abandonment to God. How often he envied her childlike faith. And she loved him—the limping cop who thought he could shield her from harm. *God, forgive me for ever placing myself in Your position of the one true protector. My arrogance has cost Allison's life.*

Beau bit back the sobs threatening to surface. *Oh, Father, forgive me for not being Your humble servant. Keep my Allison safe. Stop this madman.*

Kieron glanced at the clock. "Looks like choir is over. One of my guys had a good time following her home one night. Sorry, Pal, your pretty little girlfriend is about to meet her maker."

"I don't believe you," Beau said, masking his rage like the calmness in the eye of a storm.

"Suit yourself, but a bomb was set inside her car to explode at nine fifteen."

❧

Allison's breath caught in her throat. Someone had tried to

kill her. She stepped back from the glass doors to a wall. Whoever had put the bomb in her car could be out there watching. They didn't need to see she'd survived. Could this really be happening?

Her knees weakened, and her mind spun. She couldn't faint, not when she needed to think. Leaning against the wall, she slid to the floor and closed her eyes.

I'm safe in the shelter of God's house. But for how long?

Forcing her eyes open, she glanced around at the dimly lit foyer. A floor to ceiling cross with a huge crown of thorns caught her attention. Several yards of royal purple cloth draped around the crown and down both sides of the structure. Jesus had suffered and died for her so that she might live one day with Him—be it in the next few minutes or at another time when God saw fit to take her from this world. She could make it through what lay ahead. But what of Beau? What had happened to him?

She cringed at the thought of how he'd feel once he learned about the car bombing. He'd blame himself. Maybe she'd try calling him on his cell phone, although he probably had it turned off. And her parents. The news would devastate them. She had to make it back into the worship center and retrieve her phone.

"Allison?"

Her gaze flew to the janitor, Tom Vorder.

"What's wrong?" he asked, wobbling toward her. His eyes widened. "What is burning outside? I. . .I need to call the fire department. Has everyone gone home?" His gaze searched her face.

"Don't look at me," she said hoarsely. "Talk to me while you're staring outside at my car."

Tom paled. "Your car? Are you all right? What happened?"

"Somebody put a bomb in my car. It. . .it exploded while I was inside the worship center."

He shook his head and kept his gaze fixed outside. "I was setting up chairs for tomorrow's ladies' Bible study. With all the clanging, I didn't hear a thing."

She moistened her dry lips. "I'm so glad you're here. Look, Tom, I need to get my purse and make a couple of calls. Please keep your eyes focused on something else."

He moved toward the doors and locked them. "That ought to keep them out there."

She managed to stand on wobbly legs, using the wall for support.

"Let me get your purse," Tom said. "You don't look like you'd make it, but I'm calling the fire department and the police first. You just stay put."

"Thanks," she whispered and slid back to the floor. "My legs feel like jelly." Her heart pounded so hard it hurt.

Tom pulled out his phone and headed toward the worship center. As soon as he returned with her purse, she yanked out her phone and punched in Beau's number. Voice mail met her ears.

"Beau, somebody just blew up my car, but I'm okay." She glanced up at Tom for reassurance. "I believe the fire department and police are on their way." The older man nodded. If the pallor in his skin was any indication of how she looked, they both were in trouble.

Trembling, she called her parents. Thankfully Dad answered.

"Dad, don't panic, but my car's just been blown up. I'm safe and at church, locked inside with the janitor. The police are on their way, but I'm staying put."

"I'm coming up there!"

"No, please don't. It might be better if whoever has done this thinks I blew up with the car."

"What do you mean? What is going on?" he demanded. She heard the shaking in his voice.

"Oh, Dad, I'm not sure, but I'll explain it all to you as soon as I can. Right now I need to make another call."

"Where's Beau?" Dad asked. "Are you two in some kind of trouble? What can I do?"

"Later, Dad, please." She wanted to cry, but if she broke down, Dad would be at the church within five minutes. He'd probably come anyway. "I've got to go; I'll call you back in a little while. Just pray, okay?"

She took a deep breath and realized Tom had positioned his portly frame beside her.

"Are you going to be okay?" he asked, his face filled with concern.

She nodded. "I'm better." She offered a faint smile, and he patted her shoulder.

Allison needed to call Sergeant Landow, and with shaking fingers she found his card and phone number. He answered on the first ring.

"Sergeant Landow? This is Allison Reynolds."

"What can I do for you?" he asked, and she shakily explained what had happened. "Anyone hurt?"

"No." In the distance she could hear sirens. "The police and fire department are almost here."

"Good. I want you to stay with the officers until you hear from me or Beau. Have the officer in charge call me when he gets there."

"Yes, Sir. Is Beau all right?"

"I'm sure he is." He hung up.

She sucked in her breath, realizing the man had no idea about Beau either.

twenty

Beau's mouth tasted like cotton. Visions of Allison sped like fast-rolling film across his mind. His ears roared, and his stomach threatened to convulse. She couldn't be gone; he refused to believe it. Again, a wave of guilt and accusing whispers tore at his conscious. God forgive him. He'd killed her by his negligence, his all-consuming pride.

Gritting his teeth, he fought the despairing thoughts of Allison and what he'd done. For the moment, his attention needed to be focused on Kieron. Beau had to find a way to stop him.

A twisted smile spread over Kieron's face. He'd validated murder as if bidding on a roofing job. The head of one of the most difficult narcotics cases in Beau's history with the police department had been his neighbor and longtime friend.

Beau licked his dry lips and vowed to keep his mind alert, but every inch of him fought the desire to snap. Like billowing waves crashing against a rocky shore, adrenaline bubbled through his veins. His hands would not budge from the tape binding him, and although his backup stood outside waiting for the designated time, he wanted freedom now. His life meant nothing. All that mattered centered around stopping the animal he once called his friend.

Kieron wiped his mouth with a dirty towel. "I'm fixin' to retire," he said. "With what I've built here, I'm set for life. No one will ever suspect me. I'm just a poor guy who couldn't stand living in the big city without his precious wife."

"What are your plans?" Beau asked, twisting his wrists.

"Get rid of you. Grieve your death and bide my time before

heading to South America." He waved his hand around the room. "I won't ever have to live like this again." He picked up his phone and punched in a number. A moment later Kieron spoke to someone. "Yeah, I'm ready to bring the goods. We'll dispose of him north of town. See you in a few minutes."

"You don't have a chance, Kieron," Beau stated firmly. "The police are outside waiting."

"I doubt it. My bet goes that you kept this to yourself in hopes of prying a confession out of me," he replied, picking up the roll of duct tape. He tore a strip and wrapped it across Beau's mouth. Pulling a pocketknife from his jeans pocket, he flipped open the blade. "We're going for a little ride, but don't try anything heroic."

Beau heard the tape rip as the pocketknife sliced through to free his ankles, then around his chest where he'd been bound to the chair. With his keys in hand, Kieron opened the door leading into the garage. "I'm right behind you," he said. "Walk through that door easylike."

Beau slowly complied, but a quick shove sent him sprawling through to blackness. Whipping around, he kicked the door shut, slamming it into Kieron's face. He dashed around to the opposite side of the car. Gunfire exploded. Kieron cursed and flung open the door. Crouching by the right front wheel, Beau waited—nowhere to go.

A split moment later, the police burst through the house. Beau heard another gunshot and then the sounds of the officers handcuffing Kieron.

Beau leaned against the tire, memories of Allison tearing at his heart.

Ace shouted his name and snapped on the garage light. "Are you okay? Need some help?"

He slowly stood and emerged from the side of the car. He ignored a surge of pain in his leg and stumbled toward Ace.

"Beau's out here," he called, and opened his pocketknife to

free his hands and mouth. Ace shook his head. "Superman, you had us all worried."

Beau winced as the tape ripped out pieces of his hair and tore across his face taking a layer of skin with it. "Allison," he breathed as soon as he could speak. "Kieron said he bombed her car. Is she safe?"

"I don't know, Man," Ace said, crumbling the tape into a ball and tossing it across the garage. "But we'll find out."

Sarge appeared in the doorway. "Great job. We got him and have a lead on his buddies." He tossed Beau his cell phone. "Call Allison. She's worried sick about you. Poor lady's been through enough for one night."

"Her car?" Beau gasped.

"It's destroyed, but she was inside her church when it exploded."

"Allison's into this God-thing too?" Ace asked, furrowing his brow.

"You bet. Prayer works, Ace."

He shook his head. "Maybe it's time I listened, because working with you can be dangerous."

Beau clumsily pressed in Allison's number, shedding unashamed tears of relief. He gripped Ace's shoulder, silently thanking God for all of the night's miracles.

"You're all right," he blurted when she answered.

"Only by the grace of God," Allison said, stifling a sob. "And you? You're okay? Is it finally over?"

"Yes, Baby. I'm fine. Kieron was behind the whole thing, right from the start. The police have him in custody."

She sighed. "Kieron, your friend. I'm sorry, really I am."

"I'm the one who should be apologizing. Look at what I caused by my own stupidity."

"It doesn't matter," she said, emotion filling her words. "We can finally live again. No more threats."

He needed to see her, touch her, and make sure she hadn't

been harmed. "Where are you?"

"At the church. I never left."

~

Allison ventured up Beau's driveway and massaged her arms and shoulders. For March, the temperatures were much too cool. Spring couldn't come soon enough. She smiled, envisioning Beau's gorgeous display of flowers soon to blossom with warmer temperatures. He'd promised to give her garden tips if she kept his weeds pulled.

"Beau, where are you?" she asked, opening the gate leading to his backyard. She noted his scheferela looked healthy, and the English ivy had weathered the winter nicely.

She glanced around. He said he'd be on his patio when she arrived. She whirled around and rang his doorbell.

A pointed object poked her in the back. "You're under arrest for possession," a familiar voice muttered.

Allison laughed. "Possession of what?"

"My heart," Beau said gruffly.

"Oops. Guess I'm caught."

"Don't take this too lightly, Ma'am. This is serious business. Are you sure you want to confess to anything without an attorney? Anything you say can and will be used against you."

"I'm guilty as charged." She tried to control the laughing but gave up.

"Any last words before I handcuff you?"

"No, don't think so." She placed her hands behind her back. "Lock me up, Officer."

Beau pinned both arms behind her, making it impossible to wiggle free. Allison felt him grasp her left hand and slip something over her finger.

"This is a life sentence, you know," he whispered in her ear. His warm breath on her neck sent ripples through her body. He brushed a kiss across her shoulder, and she shivered.

"No plea-bargaining?" she whispered. "I thought undercover

policemen could work special deals?"

"Absolutely not." He released her arms and turned her to face him. Before she had a chance to look at what had been placed on her finger, he wrapped his arms around her. With a deep smile, he bent and kissed her deeply. "I love you, Allison. Will you marry me and accept a life sentence with a man who desperately needs you?"

Her heart did a double flip. "Yes, a million times yes. Without a doubt, I'm shackled to you forever."

A Letter To Our Readers

Dear Reader:

In order that we might better contribute to your reading enjoyment, we would appreciate your taking a few minutes to respond to the following questions. We welcome your comments and read each form and letter we receive. When completed, please return to the following:

Rebecca Germany, Fiction Editor
Heartsong Presents
PO Box 719
Uhrichsville, Ohio 44683

1. Did you enjoy reading *Love in Pursuit* by DiAnn Mills?
   ❏ Very much! I would like to see more books
      by this author!
   ❏ Moderately. I would have enjoyed it more if

   _____

   _____

   _____

2. Are you a member of **Heartsong Presents**?   Yes ❏ No ❏
   If no, where did you purchase this book?

   _____

3. How would you rate, on a scale from 1 (poor) to 5 (superior), the cover design?_____

4. On a scale from 1 (poor) to 10 (superior), please rate the following elements.

   _____ Heroine   _____ Plot

   _____ Hero   _____ Inspirational theme

   _____ Setting   _____ Secondary characters

5. These characters were special because_____

_____

_____

6. How has this book inspired your life?_____

_____

_____

7. What settings would you like to see covered in future **Heartsong Presents** books?_____

_____

_____

8. What are some inspirational themes you would like to see treated in future books?_____

_____

_____

9. Would you be interested in reading other **Heartsong Presents** titles?   Yes ❏   No ❏

10. Please check your age range:
    ❏ Under 18   ❏ 18-24   ❏ 25-34
    ❏ 35-45   ❏ 46-55   ❏ Over 55

Name _____

Occupation _____

Address _____

City _____ State _____ Zip _____

Email _____

CALIFORNIA

*I*n the largest, most diverse state in the Union, four women—unique in their God-given talents and goals—share a common desire to find love.

Watch as God's Spirit leads each woman to discover where true love and fulfillment are to be found. Rest in knowing that "all things work together for good to them that love God—to them who are the called according to his purpose."

paperback, 464 pages, 5 ⁳⁄₁₆" x 8"

····Hearts♥ng····

**Any 12
Heartsong
Presents titles
for only
$27.00***

CONTEMPORARY ROMANCE IS CHEAPER BY THE DOZEN!

Buy any assortment of twelve *Heartsong Presents* titles and save 25% off of the already discounted price of $2.95 each!

*plus $2.00 shipping and handling per order
and sales tax where applicable.

HEARTSONG PRESENTS *TITLES AVAILABLE NOW:*

__HP58   FREE TO LOVE, *D. English*
__HP137 DISTANT LOVE, *A. Bell*
__HP177 NEPALI NOON, *S. Hayden*
__HP178 EAGLES FOR ANNA, *C. Runyon*
__HP181 RETREAT TO LOVE, *N. Rue*
__HP182 A WING AND A PRAYER,
           T. Peterson
__HP186 WINGS LIKE EAGLES, *T. Peterson*
__HP189 A KINDLED SPARK, *C. Reece*
__HP193 COMPASSIONATE LOVE, *A. Bell*
__HP194 WAIT FOR THE MORNING,
           K. Baez
__HP197 EAGLE PILOT, *J. Stengl*
__HP201 A WHOLE NEW WORLD,
           Y. Lehman
__HP205 A QUESTION OF BALANCE,
           V. B. Jones
__HP206 POLITICALLY CORRECT,
           K. Cornelius
__HP209 SOFT BEATS MY HEART,
           A. Carter
__HP210 THE FRUIT OF HER HANDS,
           J. Orcutt
__HP213 PICTURE OF LOVE, *T. H. Murray*
__HP214 TOMORROW'S RAINBOW,
           V. Wiggins
__HP217 ODYSSEY OF LOVE,
           M. Panagiotopoulos
__HP218 HAWAIIAN HEARTBEAT,
           Y.Lehman
__HP221 THIEF OF MY HEART, *C. Bach*
__HP222 FINALLY, LOVE, *J. Stengl*
__HP225 A ROSE IS A ROSE, *R. R. Jones*
__HP226 WINGS OF THE DAWN,
           T. Peterson
__HP233 FAITH CAME LATE, *F. Chrisman*
__HP234 GLOWING EMBERS, *C. L. Reece*
__HP237 THE NEIGHBOR, *D. W. Smith*

__HP238 ANNIE'S SONG, *A. Boeshaar*
__HP242 FAR ABOVE RUBIES, *B. Melby*
           and C. Wienke
__HP245 CROSSROADS, *T. Peterson*
           and J. Peterson
__HP246 BRIANNA'S PARDON, *G. Clover*
__HP254 THE REFUGE, *R. Simons*
__HP261 RACE OF LOVE, *M. Panagiotopoulos*
__HP262 HEAVEN'S CHILD, *G. Fields*
__HP265 HEARTH OF FIRE, *C. L. Reece*
__HP266 WHAT LOVE REMEMBERS,
           M. G. Chapman
__HP269 WALKING THE DOG, *G. Sattler*
__HP270 PROMISE ME FOREVER, *A. Boeshaar*
__HP273 SUMMER PLACE, *P. Darty*
__HP274 THE HEALING PROMISE, *H. Alexander*
__HP277 ONCE MORE WITH FEELING,
           B. Bancroft
__HP278 ELIZABETH'S CHOICE, *L. Lyle*
__HP282 THE WEDDING WISH, *L. Lough*
__HP289 THE PERFECT WIFE, *G. Fields*
__HP297 A THOUSAND HILLS, *R. McCollum*
__HP298 A SENSE OF BELONGING, *T. Fowler*
__HP302 SEASONS, *G. G. Martin*
__HP305 CALL OF THE MOUNTAIN, *Y. Lehman*
__HP306 PIANO LESSONS, *G. Sattler*
__HP310 THE RELUCTANT BRIDE, *H. Spears*
__HP317 LOVE REMEMBERED, *A. Bell*
__HP318 BORN FOR THIS LOVE, *B. Bancroft*
__HP321 FORTRESS OF LOVE,
           M. Panagiotopoulos
__HP322 COUNTRY CHARM, *D. Mills*
__HP325 GONE CAMPING, *G. Sattler*
__HP326 A TENDER MELODY, *B. L. Etchison*
__HP329 MEET MY SISTER, TESS,
           K. Billerbeck
__HP330 DREAMING OF CASTLES, *G. G. Martin*
__HP337 OZARK SUNRISE, *H. Alexander*

(If ordering from this page, please remember to include it with the order form.)

....Presents....

Great Inspirational Romance at a Great Price!

Heartsong Presents books are inspirational romances in contemporary and historical settings, designed to give you an enjoyable, spirit-lifting reading experience. You can choose wonderfully written titles from some of today's best authors like Hannah Alexander, Irene B. Brand, Yvonne Lehman, Tracie Peterson, and many others.

When ordering quantities less than twelve, above titles are $3.95 each.

Not all titles may be available at time of order.

Hearts♥ng Presents
Love Stories Are Rated G!

That's for godly, gratifying, and of course, great! If you love a thrilling love story but don't appreciate the sordidness of some popular paperback romances, **Heartsong Presents** is for you. In fact, **Heartsong Presents** is the *only inspirational romance book club* featuring love stories where Christian faith is the primary ingredient in a marriage relationship.

Sign up today to receive your first set of four never-before-published Christian romances. Send no money now; you will receive a bill with the first shipment. You may cancel at any time without obligation, and if you aren't completely satisfied with any selection, you may return the books for an immediate refund!

Imagine. . .four new romances every four weeks—two historical, two contemporary—with men and women like you who long to meet the one God has chosen as the love of their lives. . .all for the low price of $9.97 postpaid.

To join, simply complete the coupon below and mail to the address provided. **Heartsong Presents** romances are rated G for another reason: They'll arrive *Godspeed!*
